Philip Hall likes me.
I reckon maybe.

by BETTE GREENE

Pictures by Charles Lilly

PUFFIN BOOKS

PUFFIN BOOKS
Published by the Penguin Group
Penguin Putnam Books for Young Readers,
345 Hudson Street, New York, New York 10014, U.S.A.
Penguin Books Ltd, 27 Wrights Lane, London W8 5TZ, England
Penguin Books Australia Ltd, Ringwood, Victoria, Australia
Penguin Books Canada Ltd, 10 Alcorn Avenue, Toronto, Ontario, Canada M4V 3B2
Penguin Books (N.Z.) Ltd, 182-190 Wairau Road, Auckland 10, New Zealand

Penguin Books Ltd, Registered Offices: Harmondsworth, Middlesex, England

First published in the United States of America by The Dial Press, 1974
Published by Puffin Books,
a member of Penguin Putnam Books for Young Readers, 1999

7 9 10 8 6

CIP IS AVAILABLE UPON REQUEST FROM THE LIBRARY OF CONGRESS.

Printed in the United States of America

For

Jordy and Carla

(and especially Carla

who never, not even once,

asked for no allergy)

OTHER PUFFIN BOOKS YOU MAY ENJOY

Contents

Philip Hall likes me.
I reckon maybe.

Philip Hall likes me.
I reckon maybe.

September

Mama set my morning bowl of steaming grits on the flowered oilcloth. "I don't want no daughter of mine filling up her head with that Hall boy today. You get yourself some learning, Beth."

I sprinkled some sugar on my grits and skimmed a spoonful from the top.

"You hear me a-speaking to you, girl?"

". . . Yes'm. But Philip Hall is my friend and—"

Mama shook her head like it almost wasn't worthwhile explaining it to me. "Beth, honey, you is so smart about most things. How come the good Lord made you so dumb about Philip Hall?"

"He didn't!" I said.

"Sure enough he did," argued Mama. "Don't you see he only wants your company if Gordy or one of them Jones boys ain't around and when he runs out of mischief to fall into?"

"Now that's not true," I said, dropping my spoon noisily into the grits. " 'Cause Philip Hall likes me. I reckon maybe. He's always inviting me over to his very own farm, now ain't that the truth?"

Ma pressed her hands against her wide waist. "That is the very thing I is speaking about," she said. "He's got you cleaning out his dairy barn—doing his work!"

"Well, I don't mind a bit," I told her. "He strummed some songs on his guitar while I worked. It was nice."

"You and your big sister better get on out of here, girl!" said Mama, wrapping her strong, dark arms around me. "Or you both going to miss the school bus." Her kiss made a smacking sound against my cheek. "Now get!"

Outside, my pa was throwing slop into the pig trough from a battered tin bucket. When he saw Anne, he called out, "EuuuuuWheee! Who that coming down the road in the starched-up dress?"

Annie smiled in that shy way she always does when she is being teased by the opposite sex. "Oh, Pa . . ."

Then Pa looked at me and asked, "Then somebody tell me who it is coming down the road in the faded jeans?"

4

"I reckon it's one of your two girl children. Want any more hints?"

"Oh, give me another little hint," said Pa, letting his good, strong teeth show.

"I'm only the daughter that's the second-best arithmetic solver, the second-best speller, and the second-best reader in Miss Johnson's class."

Pa wiped the sweat from his forehead with the sleeve of his denim shirt. "That Hall boy again? Don't go telling me he's number-one best in everything."

"Everything," I said. "Just everything." And yet Pa's question started me wondering something I never wondered before. Is Philip Hall number one only 'cause I let him be? Afraid he wouldn't like me if I were best? Shucks no! And that's too silly to even think about.

The wind was a-blowing up the dust on the dry dirt road that ran between our pig and poultry farm and Mr. Hall's dairy farm. A long time ago my mama showed me what to do when the road is dry from lack of rain and the wind comes up to make matters worse. Secret is to walk along the grass at the very edge of the road. Takes longer, but at least you can get to the highway clean.

Long after I had walked halfway, I spotted his shirt as red as dime-store lipstick. Up there where the dirt road meets up with the blacktop.

"Hey, Philip! Hey, hey, *Phil-ip!*"

He heard me because the shirt could be seen suddenly going down then up, down then up. He called out, "Run!

5

Run! Run!" As I came closer, I could see a coffee-colored arm pointing down the road in the direction that the bus comes. "Hur-ry, Hur-ry, the bus! THE BUS!"

"Let's run, Annie," I said, hugging my lunchpail and books against my chest and taking off like a turkey on Thanksgiving Eve. My sister wasn't running with me. Well, let her miss the bus if she wants to. I ran even faster down the middle of the dusty road. Five miles to school is a heap of walking. Faster, I ran faster. Running made the dust rise higher and higher. I held my breath. But suddenly my mouth opened and I sucked in air—*Ah-hm, Ahhh-hmmm—and dust.*

Philip's arms made wide circles. "Come on, Beth. Come on. Come on!"

I had to go on. Couldn't disappoint him, not sweet Philip. *Uhh chmm! Uhhhh chm!* Made myself go. Made myself run. *Uhhh hmm.* Dust in my nose. My throat. *Uhh uhhh!*

As he wildly waved me on he shouted from the loudest part of his voice, "BUS IS COMING! ALMOST HERE!"

Not much farther. I was going to make it. I had— "Ohhhhh!" A speck of something struck my right eye. If only I could lie down in the fresh grass by the side of the road, wipe the speck from my eye, and breathe country air again. But I didn't lie down, didn't stop. Kept going . . . kept running until I reached . . . reached blacktop!

After I wiped the speck from my eye, I looked down, straight down that long, blacktopped road, but I didn't see

6

anything. "Where . . . where's the bus?" I asked Philip while struggling to get back my breath.

Philip looked very serious—no, he didn't. He was biting his lip, trying to hold onto a straight face. Suddenly his lip came unbit. "Ah ha ha ha. Did I fool you! You just a-running down that road. Ah ha ha ha!"

"Why! Why! . . . You . . . you no good, low-down pole-cat!"

Philip looked surprised. "Can't you take a joke?"

I thought about shoving him into the gully at the side of the road. "That's not one bit a joke, Philip Hall. What that is is mean. Low-down mean!"

"Awww, I thought you was one girl could take a joke."

"I can!" I said, brushing the dust off me as best I could. "Just as good as anybody."

Philip nodded. "For a girl, you take jokes better than anybody." Suddenly he pointed down the road and this time the yellow bus was really on its way. He smiled a dimpled smile and I remembered why he's the cutest boy in the J. T. Williams School.

Mr. Barnes squeaked the bus to a stop and opened the door to let Fancy Annie first on board. When I got on, my friend Bonnie called, "Sit next to me, Beth."

I was just about to tell her that I had already promised to sit next to Philip Hall when I saw him slide into the seat next to Gordon. The dumb bum.

"Hey, Phil," said Gordon. "First thing this morning old Henry brought your invitation."

"Philip must be having another birthday party," whispered Bonnie. "Reckon he'll invite us?"

"Philip Hall likes me," I told her. "Most every day after my chores, I go over to his farm and he sings and just plays his guitar for me. And later this day, when old Henry gets around to our house, I reckon I'll have my invitation too."

Then Bonnie, who mostly acts as though she invented talking, stopped talking. Something had to be upsetting her, and I knew what it was. "Now don't you fret," I told her. "Maybe Philip Hall will invite you too."

"But what if he doesn't?" she asked, becoming more upset.

"Then, in that case," I told her, "don't you worry none. 'Cause you is my friend and he is my friend and I'll just tell him to invite you 'cause you is my friend."

At recess I told Susan, Ginny, and Esther about the invitation that was waiting for me. They all said that they wanted one too, and I told them all not to fret. 'Cause if they wanted to go, then I'd only have to ask Philip to invite them.

When the last bell of the day rang, I was the first one out of the classroom and third in line for the bus. Mr. Barnes isn't too good about waiting for kids and, anyway, Philip likes me to save him a place.

"Hey, Philip," I called, at the first sight of red shirt. "Over here."

Gordon looked at Philip as though he was clear out of

his mind. "You let a girl save places for you? She your girl friend, Phil?"

His face crinkled into a dark frown. "She's *not* my girl friend. And I *hate* girls!"

I climbed on the bus, without once even looking at that dumb bum who spent the whole trip back laughing with Gordon and telling him about the food they were going to eat and the games they were going to play at his birthday party. And Philip Hall is not one bit the cutest boy in school either, and that's for sure.

Where our dirt road meets the blacktop, Mr. Barnes brought the bus to a stop and Anne, Philip, and I jumped off. As my boy friend no more and I poked along the dirt road together, I wasn't saying one word to him. Finally, he said something to me, "Afternoon shower dampened the road down. Ain't one bit dusty now."

"Reckon I'm not going to talk to you about any damp roads or any dusty roads or any kind of roads at all."

Philip dimpled a smile. "Oh, you is mad, Beth Lambert. You is mad, Mad, MAD! Ain't that right?"

"That is right, Mister Philip best-in-the-class Hall. You all the time rather be sitting with Gordon and laughing with Gordon and telling him that I'm not your friend. And that makes me mad. Mad. Mad. MAD!"

Philip reached up and pulled a leaf from an elm. "You is my friend all right."

"I am . . . truly?"

Philip looked down at his shoes and nodded. "Sure. 'Cause after you finish up the chores on your farm, I'm going to let you come visit. I'm going to let you brush down my cows."

"See you directly," I called as I started running to catch up with Anne. My chores shouldn't take long. And then probably I could go over to Philip Hall's. Sweet Philip. I had to get him something very special for his eleventh birthday. What?

Suddenly I knew. A pick for his guitar just like they sell at the Busy Bee Bargain Store. And with the nickel I had saved from not buying ice cream last Saturday, together with the nickel that Pa will give me this Saturday, then I'd have a whole dime to spend on a guitar pick for sweet Philip Hall.

Mama was sitting on her porch chair, rocking away. Near her feet was the big sewing basket and in her lap was Pa's old overalls that was getting fresh knee patches.

"Hey, Ma, old Henry brought the mail yet?"

She looked up from her sewing. "Mail's on the kitchen table."

Behind me, I heard the screen door slam. Mama don't like no screen door slamming. On the oilcloth-covered table was a platter of fried chicken, a pot of still warm black-eyed peas, and a catalog for mail ordering. This ain't all the mail. Can't be!

I went back into the living room, which is also my

brother Luther's bedroom, and hollered through the screen door, "Ma, this ain't all the mail . . . is it?"

She was quiet for a moment and I thought she was about to say that was all there was when, "No-o-o," she called back, "reckon not. There's something else on my bureau."

I knew it. I just knew it! But when I looked the only piece of mail I saw was a circular announcing bargain day at the Busy Bee. Maybe the invitation is underneath. Sure. My hand touched the sheet of advertisement without really moving it. I hope, I hope. I lifted the circular. And there was—nothing! Absolutely nothing.

I tiptoed out the kitchen door, closing it without a sound. Crossed the dirt road, shortcutted through the cornfield and past the mailbox where the sign read: HALL'S DAIRY. Inside the barn Philip was sitting on a bale of hay, picking out a tune on his guitar.

Without even looking up from his guitar strings, he said, "You better get busy, Beth. You got eight milk cows to brush down today."

"You didn't send me one." My voice sounded right next door to tears.

Philip took notice. "What? Send you—"

"A birthday invitation," I said. "Sent one to Gordon, but not to me."

"Oh," said Philip. "That. That's what you mad about?"

I nodded while tears stung at my eyes. "I was going to

buy you a special present 'cause I thought you was my friend, but you're not my friend at all."

"Don't be like that," he said. "I didn't invite girls, only Gordy, Bobby, and Jordan and Joshua Jones—the brave members of the Tiger Hunters' Club. We're the boys ain't afraid of nothing. Not even roaring mad tigers."

"Well, why couldn't you invite me too? I'm not even a little bit afraid of tigers either and you said . . . this very day, you said I was your friend."

Philip nodded his head yes.

"So why didn't you invite me too?"

". . . I can't."

"Well why not?"

"Just can't."

"Why *not?*"

"Just *can't* do it."

"*Why!?*"

" 'Cause."

" 'Cause *why?*"

" 'Cause . . . 'cause I was afraid they'd call me sissy. Then they'd go 'round saying I liked you and that you was my girl friend, stuff like that."

"And you the president of the Tiger Hunters?" I asked. "That the club ain't afraid of nothing, not even roaring mad tigers?" I began to laugh.

Philip looked frightened. "What you laughing at?"

I only laughed some more.

"Are you laughing at me?"

"Reckon I is 'cause you is funny, Funny, FUNNY, Mister Philip Hall."

"I'm not! Not! NOT!" shouted Philip, jumping off the bale of hay.

"Oh, yes you is. You say you ain't afraid of tigers. Well, I don't know a soul ever seen a tiger, not in all of Randolph County. But you is afraid of a word, and everybody knows that words can't bite and words can't scratch. So you're not a tiger hunter, Philip Hall. What you is, is a 'fraidy cat. And that's a whole lot worse than being a sissy."

The next day was Thursday and Ma said I looked sickly so she kept me home from school. And on Friday she said the same thing and kept me home again.

On Saturday Philip had his birthday party. I saw the Tiger Hunters being driven over by Gordon's pa in their blue pickup truck. I kept telling myself to be happy. After all, I wouldn t have to spend perfectly good ice-cream money on a stupid guitar pick for that low-down dumb bum of a polecat. But truth of the matter is, I wasn't happy. Wasn't happy at all.

By noontime, Ma, Pa, my brother Luther, my sister Anne, and I had all eaten, washed, and got fancy dressed for town. At the Busy Bee, I saw Bonnie, who turned her head the moment she saw me, just as if she was mad.

"Bonnie! Hey!"

"I'm *not* about to speak to you," she said, turning to face me. "You promised you'd get Phil to invite me to his birthday party, didn't you? Didn't you promise?"

"He didn't invite me either," I told her.

Bonnie's eyes grew big and round. "But you is his best friend."

"No more," I said. "I haven't been over to his farm for three days."

"After school on Monday," said Bonnie, "you come on over to my farm." Suddenly she pointed a finger at my nose. "You can be my friend, OK?"

"OK," I said. "OK."

When the last school bell of the day rang on Monday, Bonnie and I grabbed hands and ran out of Miss Johnson's classroom. Philip and Gordon were already waiting in the bus line.

"Hey, Beth!" called Philip. "Over here. I saved a place for you."

Gordon looked shocked. "What are you saving places for girls for?"

Philip looked Gordon straight in the eye. "Because I want to—that's what for."

"Is you a sissy?" asked Gordon, suddenly putting his hands on his hips. "With girl friends?"

"Something worse than being a sissy," said Philip, "is being a 'fraidy cat. And from this day on, any Tiger Hunter who is afraid of girls ain't going to be called a Tiger

Hunter anymore." Then Philip stuck his face so close to Gordon's that their noses touched. "And do you know what we're going to call them kind of Tiger Hunters?"

Gordon moved his face away while shaking his head no.

"Them kind we call 'Fraidy Cats," said Philip, looking from Gordon to me. It was as though he wanted to know if I liked what he was saying.

I felt myself smiling.

Gordon took a couple of steps backward, opening a large space in line. "You girls can get in front of me," he said.

Philip smiled his happiest smile. Sweet Philip. The cutest boy in the J. T. Williams School and the bravest Tiger Hunter of them all.

Case of
the missing turkeys

December

Miss Johnson was telling the class that never in the whole history of schoolteaching had there ever been such a perfectly wonderful number-one best student as me. Philip Hall rushed to congratulate me, "I likes you even better now than I did when you were only number two."

So much happiness rushed to my heart that it had to expand to mite near twice its usual size just to take it all in. Then *Bang! Bang! Bang!* My eyes snapped open at the early morning noise outside my bedroom window while at the same moment, Miss Johnson, Philip Hall, and my dream—my beautiful dream—dissolved like a raindrop into a freshly plowed field.

Minutes later I carried my breakfast of a cup of sweet milk and a slab of cornbread to where Pa was hammering one of the steel fence poles deeper into the ground. Even though December had been around for better'n a week, Pa was sweating under the Arkansas sun. His face looked as polished as black shoes on a Sunday morning.

He didn't answer to "Morning, Pa." Only muttered that he didn't know how it was happening, but he didn't intend for it to continue.

I said, "None of your turkeys disappeared during the night." But when Pa still didn't answer, I made a question out of it. "Did any of your turkeys disappear during the night?"

He wiped his forehead with a red bandanna. "Another ten, maybe more."

"Oh, Pa," I said, taking on some of the burden. "We were so sure that all those strips of cloths flapping from the fence would scare off the chicken hawks."

"Ain't no hawk with the sense God gave him gonna mess around with no twenty-pound turkey."

I had another idea. "If a hawk won't, a fox will. And we got plenty of red foxes slying around these parts."

His forehead furrowed. "That fox would have to crawl under this fence, which is pretty dang smart seeing as there ain't no crawl-through space."

"Maybe he went over?" I suggested.

"Over six-feet-high fencing? Not unless them red foxes is taking flying lessons."

When I mentioned that there are other ways to get inside a turkey yard—such as climbing over the fence—Pa nodded, threw open the gate, and told me to go inside the yard, get down on all fours, and pretend to be a hungry red fox.

With my height cut in half, the fence looked twice as high. But never mind that. How can I, the fox, get back over that fence with six or more of Farmer Lambert's plumpest turkeys? Pa watched carefully as I carefully thought. Finally I gave up. "A fox couldn't get back over that fence with the turkeys so he'd have to do what folks in restaurants do. Eat their turkey dinner on the premises."

"Spoken like a true fox," said Pa. "Which proves it wasn't no fox 'cause there ain't no blood or bones—no turkey remains of any kind in this here yard."

The next thing I thought of was a groundhog who tunnels his way inside the fencing and then drags off the turkeys through miles and miles of winding underground passageways.

"It makes about as much sense as any other explanation," said Pa as we walked across every foot of the turkey yard in search of the mouth to the passageway.

I found the blue button missing from my winter coat and Pa found Luther's nineteen-cent mechanical pencil, but nobody found no tunnel opening.

He leaned back against the range shelter and sighed.

"Don't make no more sense suspecting a groundhog than it do in suspecting the Easter bunny."

I sighed back, when suddenly an idea struck with such force that I knew that the mystery wasn't going to be a mystery no more. Pointing toward the turkey compound, I said, "An airplane!"

Pa looked. "Where?"

"Nowhere there. I'm saying an airplane is making our birds disappear."

"An airplane," he repeated, laughing first a little and then harder and harder. Every time I told him to quit his laughing and let me explain, he'd only laugh harder. I gave him a little poke to the ribs.

"Now you listen to me, Pa! I might know something that can save our turkeys."

And when I said that, Pa seemed to lose his laughter. "Then speak on, Beth girl, speak on."

"Well, pretend this plane has left New York City and is flying west. The pilot has to take his plane up higher to get over our Ozark Mountains, but once over the mountains, the plane swoops back down low, right over this farm. Right over this turkey yard!"

"So-o-o," said Pa. "You is think—"

"I is thinking," I said, interrupting, "that some mighty low-flying airplanes is scaring our poultry into taking to the air."

I watched Pa's lips shape themselves into a near perfect O. "Scared-enough turkeys could have flown over that fence

—sure could—and come to roost in some nearby trees."

We searched the branches of every tree from here to the highway. I found a bees' nest in one and Pa found one of Ma's missing facecloths in another, but neither of us found a single turkey resting on a single limb.

"Should 'ave known better'n blaming some airplane," said Pa, rubbing the back of his neck. " 'Cause even if planes had scared them into some nighttime tree roosting, by morning feeding time they'd be knocking the compound's fence down trying to get back in."

When we came in to eat, Ma was already putting chicken salad (always made with turkey in our house), sliced tomatoes, cornbread, and tall glasses of cold, fresh buttermilk on the table. She took one look at Pa and reminded him that he ain't the first farmer to spoil a crop or lose a bird. "So wash up and eat up," she said. " 'Cause we're going into town for some trading and socializing."

On Pocahontas's Main Street, Pa angle-parked directly in front of Calvin's Meat Market, where Calvin Cook, his fat son Calvin Junior, Miss Elinor Linwood, and Sheriff Nathan Miller weren't, truth to tell, arguing so much as they were engaged in spirited conversation. The sheriff shook his head as though he was trying to shake off the nonsense. "I ain't for a moment doubting that you saw something, Miss Linwood. I'm only doubting that what you saw was the Monster of the Mountain."

Miss Linwood's eyes seemed to be lit from inside. "He

was half again as tall as any man. Eight, maybe nine feet tall. I never saw his face, but I saw his hands, and they were big enough for carrying all manner of things."

Ma pushed me on. "Listening in on other folks' conversation ain't considered proper. Didn't I learn you that?"

But proper or not, everybody all up and down Main Street seemed to be talking about nothing but Miss Linwood's sighting of the Monster of the Mountain. Over the years very few people have claimed seeing him, but there wasn't hardly nobody that didn't have a favorite Monster of the Mountain story to tell.

Our minister, the Reverend Ross, was remembering the night way back in 1938 when the Ringling Bros. and Barnum & Bailey Circus train derailed five miles west of Pocahontas. "State police from three states searched the Ozarks for miles around without letting any of us home folks know what it was they were searching for."

"Reckon that's where the Monster of the Mountain came from?" I asked.

He pulled a flat toothpick from his black suit and stuck it between his front teeth. "Don't know that for bible-preaching sure, but I do know this: Gorilla Man was the circus's feature attraction before the derailment, but afterwards he was never exhibited again."

When we got back to the farm, Ma and Anne went right into the house saying they was too tired to do anything but fall into bed while Luther did exactly what he always does when he hasn't seen his precious pigs in a few hours. "Got to go ask them if they missed me," Luther said with his grin.

Lots of times I've asked my brother whether he sure-to-goodness believes that pigs could miss any human person. And he always answers, "Shore," while holding onto his little grin. And then I'd say, "Now, Luther, you tell me the God's honest truth. Do you really, really *believe* that?"

Tonight when I asked him, Luther pointed a finger at me, which suddenly made him look a lot older than fourteen. "When you is old enough to know, Miss Beth baby, I'm going to tell you."

"I'm old enough to know right now," I said, suddenly hearing the sounds of smart aleck in my voice.

As he walked toward the pig pen, he called over his shoulder, "When you is really old enough to know, you already will."

The night was cold and morning a long time coming. Once during my sleep I woke, thinking I heard the untamed cry of Gorilla Man.

At the breakfast table Pa, already Sunday-dressed in his good suit and polka-dot tie, sat smiling like he was real pleased with himself as he dropped spoons of sugar on top of a huge steaming bowl of oatmeal. As I sat down, he was too busy explaining how he outwitted the low-down turkey thief with a few well-placed kerosene lanterns to take any notice.

Ma noticed though and right away went to the pot to

ladle me out a bowl before she turned to look at Pa. "Eugene Lambert, you haven't been out to check on your flock yet and you, of all folks, oughta know better'n counting your turkeys before they is counted."

"Even the devil don't go messing around no place that's light," said Pa, already beginning to back out the kitchen door.

Just as I began thinking that at last Pa had put a stop to the disappearings, he came back through the back door looking as strange as he would if a dozen men from a far-off planet came floating through our kitchen to ask directions.

"Eugene," shouted Ma, rushing to his side. "Are you ailing?"

He shook his head with such force that I was sure he was only trying to shake off his troubles. "Another six—maybe more—missing!"

Ma clasped her hands. "Lord, don't tell me."

"How's a man suppose to earn a living?" asked Pa, making it sound more like a complaint than a question. " 'Cause the chicken hawk, red fox, groundhog, airplane, or whatever the critter calls himself, ain't one bit fooled by me. So what's a man to do?"

As soon as we came home from church, Pa took out his letter paper and wrote to the Answer Man at his favorite magazine, *Turkey World*. As he licked the envelope closed, he spoke directly to me, "I gave them folks at the

magazine all the facts I know. Reckon they can figger out what's happening?"

"Sure, Pa. Ever know the Answer Man not to have the answers?"

"Never," said Pa, perking up. "I don't remember there ever being a question that the Answer Man couldn't answer, not in all the fifteen years that I've had a prescription."

"Subscription," I corrected. "Prescription is what Doc Brenner gives you when you're ailing."

He stood up to give me little pitty-pats to the top of my head. "Ooooo—eeee, ain't I got me some smart girl? Is you sure that Hall boy is the number-one best student?"

But by the time I answered No, sir, that I wasn't sure, not completely, Pa had already turned his attention to Ma, saying, "I'm going to spend this night guarding the turkey range. Only thing I know to do until the Answer Man tells me better."

At daybreak I woke when Pa came into the house mumbling, "Safe tonight. I kept them safe tonight." Then he dropped to his bed so hard that I heard the bedsprings strike the floor. And it was then that I heard my mother's voice saying, "That's the last time you is going to do that, Mister Eugene Lambert."

But the closest Pa came to answering was a steady ZZZZ zzzz ZZZZZZ zzz.

The next day at recess I got Philip Hall aside and begged him to help me this very night to solve the mystery of the missing turkeys. He shook his head saying, "We'll have to put it off for a spell. Some things ain't safe to do so soon after the Monster of the Mountain has been seen about."

When I told him that I didn't think that Tiger Hunters were supposed to be afraid of monsters, Philip seemed to remember that that was true. Then he even reminded me that he himself wasn't afraid. "Not a bit."

I waited until our house darkened and filled with sleep sounds before getting out of bed. Outside the air felt as though it had been refrigerated, and an orange ball of a moon looked just about perfect for throwing illumination on Barnum & Bailey's long-lost Gorilla Man.

That thought made me want to rush back into the house, but other thoughts kept me from doing it. Thoughts about what would happen to all us Lamberts if Pa's turkeys went on disappearing, thoughts about brave Philip waiting for me down by the turkey compound, and there was still one more thought. And this was the cheeriest one of all: Sheriff Miller saying right out loud that the only place the Monster of the Mountain lived was in some folks' imagination.

But just to be on the safe side, I crossed everything that it was possible to cross as I tiptoed deeper into the darkness toward the poultry range gate. When I reached the thick-trunked tree, Philip wasn't waiting there. I told myself not to fret as I climbed up the tree. He'll be along directly. Didn't he promise me, not once but twice, that he'd sneak out just as soon as everybody in his house was asleep?

As I began to find comfort in believing that sweet Philip was right now on his way over, it happened. God switched off his nightlight and the whole earth was plunged from moonlight to nolight. Fear struck against the inside of my chest like a fighter's fist.

I held my hand over my heart as I looked to the sky. Only a black rain cloud passing before the moon. When the moonlight returned, I felt better. You is some baby, Beth Lambert, I told myself.

Then from over Philip's way, a light—it was a flashlight poking bright spots into the darkness. I was at a far enough distance from the house to give out one of my tongue-curled-behind-my-front-teeth whistles. He heard because right away he flashed the light onto his face and body. Philip was wearing the complete Boy Scout uniform, even down to the sash that crossed his chest and served as a showplace (as well as a sticking place) for all six of his merit badges.

When he reached my tree, he handed up his flashlight and his battered BB gun for me to hold until he seated himself into the Y-shaped branch opposite mine. "Your pa's turkeys are going to sleep tight tonight," he said, patting the barrel of his gun. " 'Cause I'm a-going to shoot anything that moves."

After a while the snug branches that cradled me began to feel more like a branch than a cradle. Philip didn't seem to mind the hardness, though; maybe it was because he was all the time complaining another complaint. He was real cold. I didn't blame him much. The wind was whipping through the ice-glazed branches. But wouldn't you think that silly Scout would have known enough to wear a coat?

Suddenly a wild *OHHHhh—ooooo* shattered and splattered the quiet. *OHHhhh—oooooo.*

Philip grabbed my arm. "G-G-G-Gorilla Man?"

"No, only a love-sick coyote," I told him, wondering if there would ever come a time when he'd hold onto my arm without being frightened into it.

"I guess I know that!" he said, releasing my arm. Then he warned me that I was going to have to stay calm and collected.

"I'll try."

"Good," he said. " 'Cause I can shoot any chicken hawk or fox that gets behind that fence."

I asked, "That the same gun that couldn't knock over a tin can?"

"It did too!"

"Yeah, but not until you were so close your breath could have done it."

Philip began telling me that I didn't know nothing, "Nothing at all!" But he stopped fussing the moment I touched his arm and pointed to a moving vehicle that had just turned off the main highway onto the dirt road dividing the Lambert Pig and Poultry Farm from the Hall Dairy Farm. And since the only place the old rutted road could take a person is to our farm or Philip's, I asked him if his folks were expecting visitors.

"Our house been sleeping for quite a spell," he answered, turning to look at our lightless house. "Yours too?"

I nodded yes, wondering if nods can be seen by moonlight.

The vehicle, which began to look more and more like a truck, cut its lights while continuing to move through the darkness.

"Why—why—?" Philip asked, as he began squeezing the blood from my hand. "Why, why did . . . why did . . . why—"

"Did they do that," I said, filling in the question for him before answering it. "I don't know."

The panel truck circled our tree before coming to a stop at the turkey-yard gate. Both doors opened and two people —both men—got out and without a single word lifted the latch and entered the compound.

Then from Philip's mouth came little pops of breath.

"Shhhh . . ."

Pop/pop/pop/pop/pop/pop.

I threw my hand across his mouth. "Hush," I said into his ear. "I'm going to be needing your help, you hear?" When I felt his face bob up and down, I let go of his mouth. "Sneak on into our house. Wake Pa and Luther while I see if I can recognize those thieves."

Philip handed me his gun while he shimmied down the tree's backside.

I watched the men with their long, white cotton-picker's sacks move on toward the roosting turkeys. Through the moonlight I strained my eyes trying to see just who they were. I couldn't. But I did hear me a heap of flapping and gobbling going on. Under my breath I said, "Come on, Pa. Oh, please!" But what if they take off with two bags full of turkeys before Pa and Luther get here? Then we'd never know who's to blame . . . unless . . . unless—the license plate!

Still holding onto Philip's gun, I climbed down the tree and edged around to the rear of the panel truck. I couldn't see the numbers so I brailled it. Seven . . . nine . . . four . . . two . . . six . . . five. Just as I began congratulating myself on the fact that I now had those crooks' license number, I discovered that I couldn't remember it. Excepting that it started with a five, or was it a six?

I looked back over to our house, which was as black as a coal stove's innards. "Oh, Pa," I said, making it sound more like a prayer than a request. "Where are you when I need you?"

Then I saw them pulling their now-filled canvas bags toward the gate. Like a chant, I kept saying the word, "Pa . . . Pa . . . Pa . . ." But our house slept on, dark as ever.

As a hand clicked the gate's latch, I shouted, "Stay where you is!" While my own hand kept groping for the trigger. Where is that trigger?

"*What!*" shouted a duet of voices.

Finally I found it. "I said, stay where you are before I shoot you full of lead!"

"Pop, don't let me be shot!" screamed one man, who turned out to be an overgrown boy.

"Shut your mouth, Calvin Junior."

So that's who it is. The Calvin Cooks. Junior and Senior.

"Well, well," said the butcher, trying for a light note. "Why don't you put that hunting rifle down before you go hurting yourself?"

In the moonlight he had mistaken the BB gun for a rifle.

"Look, we're sorry we bothered you." He touched the latch. "Well, we'll be leaving now."

I used my meanest voice. "First one touches that gate is the first one going to get shot."

Then in the distance a door slammed and heavy feet began running my way, snapping branches and breaking twigs.

"Pa!" I called into the night. "Here! Over here!"

Within moments, he came to my side with a sudden sliding stop. His powerful hunting rifle was aimed directly at Calvin Cook Senior as he asked me, "You all right?"

My strength felt as though it had all been used up. Still I was able to manage, "I'm OK-K-K."

When Luther, Ma, and Philip Hall came running up,

Pa moved his rifle up and down at the Cooks saying, "Would you look what strange-looking birds Beth found in our turkey yard."

"It's the Cooks from the meat market," I said as Philip flashed his flashlight on them. Neither one of them Cooks seemed to appreciate the spotlight.

Mr. Cook moved his hands into a let's-be-friends gesture. "Now there's no harm done so you'd just better let us go now."

"Don't you go talking about no harm," answered Pa. "You've been taking our hard-earned living away from us! What do you know or care about the harm you caused?"

One of the turkeys found its way out of a long canvas bag and with a good loud squawk ran off in the direction of the range shelter.

Mr. Cook forced a smile as he pulled out a thick wad of money and slid off one of the bills before handing it out toward Pa. "All right, I don't blame you a bit for wanting something. So here's five dollars for your trouble."

Pa took the money. "Reckon this oughta pay me for one of my turkeys, but them's forty-nine others needing to be paid for."

"*What!*" shouted the butcher. "Your turkeys aren't worth five dollars apiece. Why, I never sold a single one of them for more than four dollars—or maybe four-fifty apiece."

"Mister, I reckon you better peel off another forty-nine of those five dollar bills."

Mr. Cook pointed his finger at Pa. "Why, that's highway robbery!"

Pa nodded his head in agreement. "That's just what we is talking about. You coming off that highway to rob me . . . Luther, drive the truck over to Sheriff Miller's house. Tell him to get right over here and arrest these low-down critters."

"Wait up now. Wait up!" said the butcher, whose hands gave up their pointing to return to a more friendly motion. That being the motion of peeling off five dollar bills and handing them over to Pa. When the forty-ninth bill was counted, Mr. Cook reached for the latch.

"Stay put," said Pa, jiggling his rifle before turning to Luther. "Didn't I tell you to get the sheriff? Didn't I tell you that?"

Almost at the moment that Luther said, "But I thought —" Mr. Cook screamed, *"What!"*

From down the highway came a speeding car with a flashing dome light and the long, low wail of a siren. A minute later Sheriff Nathan Miller snapped the steel handcuffs around the wrists of the Cooks. "Farmers hereabout been complaining about missing livestock ever since you Cooks moved into town."

Calvin Junior's lower lip pouted forward as he spoke directly to me. "All this is your fault! My daddy's a respectable businessman."

"Respect don't keep company with greed."

Calvin Junior went on, "You oughta be ashamed of yourself, a girl carrying a dangerous rifle."

"And that's twice you is wrong," I said, holding up the BB gun so he could get a better look. "Don't reckon I could tell you which would be more painful, getting shot by this BB gun or running head on into a mosquito."

It was then that the rest of the turkeys found their way out of the Cooks' canvas bags and with squawks of victory ran off through the darkness.

I never
asked for no allergy

February

Mr. Barnes stopped the school bus along the side of the highway just at that spot where the dirt road leading to our farm meets the blacktop. First Philip Hall got off. Then I jumped off in front of the faded black-and-white sign at the intersection which read:

1 mile
↑
Lambert Farm
good turkeys
good pigs

As I took a flying leap across the frozen drainage ditch that separated the road from the field, I heard Philip calling me.

"Hey, Beth!" He was still standing on the blacktop just where the bus left him. "You oughtna be going through the field. You might step into an ice puddle."

Of all days to have to stop and start explaining things to Philip Hall. But at any other time I'd be thinking that he wouldn't be fretting about my feet if he didn't really like me. Now would he? "Frosty feet ain't nothing," I told him. "When you have a spanking new puppy waiting to meet you."

"What if Mr. Grant wouldn't swap a collie dog for one of your pa's turkeys?" asked Philip, grinning as though he hoped it was so.

"That's all you know! When I left the house this morning, my pa was picking out six of our fattest turkeys for swapping." I turned and began running across the field.

"Well, one collie dog is worth more than six of your old turkeys," called Philip.

I kept on running, pretending not to hear. And, anyway, everybody loves to eat turkey. Don't they?

When I reached the rise in the field, I could see our house a nice pale green. It always surprised me a little to see the house painted because until last year the weathered boards had never ever seen a lick of paint.

That was the year Pa sold mite near three hundred turkeys not even speaking about the forty-two pigs. And that was when Pa asked Ma what it was she wanted most. And she said that all her life she had wanted to live in a painted house. Especially in a house that was painted green.

As I came closer, I could see the chocolate brownness of my mama against the paleness of the porch. She was hanging work-worn overalls across the porch clothesline. Ma used to always be finished with the laundry by this time of day, but she says that carrying a baby inside tends to slow a person down a mite.

I tiptoed up behind her and threw my arms as far as they would go, which was about half the distance around her ever-widening waist.

"Ohhh!" She jumped. "What you mean scaring me clear out of my wits, girl?"

"Where is he?" I asked. "Where's the collie?"

She put on her I'm-not-fixing-to-listen-to-any-nonsense face and said, "I don't know nothing about no collie."

"Did Pa make the swap? Did he?"

"Get out of here, girl. Go on into the kitchen."

"Tell me if Pa got the collie," I pleaded. "Now did he?"

Her mouth was still set into that no-nonsense way of hers, but it was different with her eyes. Her eyes were filled up with pure pleasure. "And I told you," she said, "to get on into the kitchen, didn't I?"

Suddenly I understood. I threw open the screen door and, without waiting to close it gently behind me, ran in a straight line through the living room and into the kitchen.

And then I saw him. There in a cardboard carton next

to the cookstove was a reddish-brown puppy with a circle of white fluffy hair ringing his neck and spilling down to his chest. I dropped to my knees and showed my open palms. "Hi, puppy. Beautiful little collie puppy."

"He's beautiful, sure enough," said Ma from behind.

The collie just looked at me for a few moments. Then he got to his feet and trotted over.

"And you're friendly too," I said, patting his back. "Hey, that would be a good name for you."

"Friendly," said Ma, smacking her lips like she was word tasting. "That's a right good name."

I gave Friendly a hug and a kiss. "I will now name you —*ah-choo!*" I tried again. "I will now name—*AHHHH-hhhhh-choo!!*"

Ma shook her head the way she does when she catches me at mischief. "You done gone and got yourself a cold, now, didn't you?"

"*AHHHHhhhhhh-ha-ha-ha-choo!* I now name you Friendly," I said at last.

By bedtime I was sneezing constantly and water kept pouring from my sore, itchy eyes. But, thank goodness, all my sneezing didn't seem to bother Friendly, who slept peacefully in his cardboard carton at the foot of my bed.

I could hear my folks in the kitchen talking about what they were always talking about these days—names for our soon-to-be-born baby. When they finally tired of that topic, Ma said, "Beth got me worried. All them wheezing sounds coming from her chest."

"I seen Doc Brenner in town this afternoon," said Pa. "He asked me to kill and clean one of our twenty-pound birds. Said he'd stop by this evening to pick it up."

"When he comes by," said Ma, "ask him to kindly take a look at our Beth."

I climbed out of bed to take off my raggedy tail of a nightgown and put on the one that Grandma had given me last Christmas. She had made it out of a sack of Fairy Flake flour, but she dyed it a bright, brilliant orange. It was nice.

Friendly started to bark.

"Don't you be frightened, little Friendly, it's only me, only Beth."

While I patted my new pet, I told him how glad I was that he had come to live with us. "You're going to like it here, you'll see. I'm going to bring all my friends to meet you. Philip Hall, Susan, Bon—*ahh-choo-whoo! Ahh choo!* Bonnie, Ginny, Esther. You're going to like all my friends, Friendly, but you're going to like me best of all . . . I reckon maybe."

Ma called out, "Is you out of bed, Beth?"

I jumped back into bed before answering. "No m'am, I'm right here. Right here in bed."

I kept my eyes open, waiting for the doctor to come, but after a while my eyelids came together. Sleep stood by waiting for me to fall . . . fall asleep . . . sleep . . . sleep.

"Let me take a look at my old friend, Beth," said a big voice.

My cheeks were being patted. "Doctor's here, Beth honey," Ma was saying.

I pulled myself up to sitting and looked into the face of Dr. Brenner, who said, "This won't hurt," as he placed a freezing stethoscope to my chest.

I jumped. "It's cold."

He rubbed the stethoscope warm with his hands. "That doesn't sound much like the Beth Lambert who caught those turkey-thieving Cooks with only a"—Doc Brenner commenced laughing—"with only a . . ." But again his laughing interfered with his talking so I just said, "With only a BB gun," while the doctor laughed all the harder.

After wiping away all the tears that his laughter shook loose, Doctor Bernard M. Brenner became fully professional. "Just breathe naturally," he said as he put the warmed tube back to my chest. He listened quietly without saying a word. Then he took the stethoscope from his ears. "I heard some wheezing sounds coming from your chest. Tell me, how do your eyes feel?"

"They feel like I want to grab them out of their sockets and give them a good scratching. They're so . . . so itchy."

"Uh-hun," answered Dr. Brenner, as though he knew all about itchy eyes. "Beth, can you remember when all this sneezing and wheezing began?"

Across the room, my sister turned over in her bed and

let out a groan without once opening her eyes. It was as if Anne was making a complaint that her sleep was being disturbed by inconsiderate folks.

"Yes, sir," I told the doctor. "It all started when I met Friendly."

Friendly must have heard his name called 'cause he jumped out of his carton and jogged floppily on over.

"Hi, little Friendly, little dog." I picked him up and gave him a hug and a kiss. *"AHHHHhh—choo! Ah-choo!"*

"Beth," said Dr. Brenner, running his fingers through his silver hair. "I'm sorry to do this, but I'm going to have to tell you something. Something you're not going to like hearing. I believe you have an allergy to Friendly."

"Oh, no sir, I don't!" I cried. "I don't have one, honest. I never asked for no allergy. Why, I don't even know what that means."

Dr. Brenner took my hand. "It simply means that Friendly's dog hair is making you sick. And, furthermore, it means that he must be returned to wherever he came from."

"But Friendly is *my* dog. He belongs to me. And he's never *never* going to go back to that kennel!" I felt tears filling up my eyes. "I love Friendly; Friendly loves me."

"I know you love one another," agreed Dr. Brenner. "But all this sneezing, wheezing, and red eyes is your body's way of telling you something."

I shook my head no.

Doc Brenner nodded his head yes. "Bodies don't need to say fancy words like allergic rhinitis—or any words at all, Beth. When your throat is dry, you don't wait to hear the word *water* before taking a drink. And do you really need the school's lunch bell to ring before you know when it's time to eat? Well, now your body is saying something just as important. Listen to it!" he said, cupping his hand around his ear. But the only sound in the room was the hissing noise coming from my own chest.

When the morning sun came flooding through my bedroom window, my eyes opened and I remembered about the allergy. Was it real or only a dream?

"Friendly," I called. "Come here, little Friendly."

But Friendly didn't come and I didn't hear him either. I jumped to the foot of my bed. The cardboard box was empty. They've taken him back to Mr. Grant's kennel!

I was just about to shout out for Friendly when outside the kitchen window I heard Luther's and Anne's voices: "Get that ball, Friendly. Friendly, you going to get that ball?"

Ma laughed. "That dog ain't fixing to do nothing he ain't a mind to do."

I went out the kitchen door still wearing my orange nightgown and sat down on the back steps next to her. She put her arm around me and gave me a quick squeeze. "How you feeling, honey babe?"

I thought about her question. My chest felt as though it

was still filled up with old swamp water while my head carried around last night's headache. Finally, I gave my answer, "I'm OK, Mama. I reckon."

"After you come home from school, I want you to take a little nap. Never mind them chores, just put your head down on the pillow and nap. 'Cause you spent half the night crying into your pillow."

"About what the doctor said . . . about taking Friendly back to the kennel. We're not going to listen to that, are we?"

She looked past me, out to where Luther and Anne were playing with Friendly. "Life don't always be the way we want it to be. Life be the way it is. Ain't nothing we can do."

"You *can't* take him back!" I shouted. "Besides, Mr. Grant probably's eaten up all the turkeys."

"If he did, he did," answered Ma.

"You don't understand," I said, bringing my voice back down to size. "I *need* Friendly! Luther was three and Anne was two when I was born so they had me, but I never had nothing little and soft to—"

"And I told you," she said, "that life be the way it be. Ain't nothing we can do. But if you misses that school bus, there is something I can do. I can take a switch to you. So *get!*"

At school I felt better and worse. Better because I didn't sneeze or wheeze and even my eyes stopped itching and watering. And worse because tonight, after supper,

Friendly was going back to Mr. Grant's kennel.

If only I had some magic. One time I remembered my teacher, Miss Johnson, pointing to shelves of books and saying that they held many secrets. Could one of her books hold the secret of making the allergy go and the dog stay?

At recess, she stood on a three-step ladder to bring down a heavy book from the top shelf.

"This book may have the secret we're looking for," she said, pointing to a page. "Right here," she whispered, the way people do when they're telling secrets. "It says that people who have an allergy to long-haired dogs, like the collie, might not have an allergy to a short-haired dog, like the chihuahua."

At the kennel I held Friendly close to me while Pa explained about the allergy to Mr. Grant.

"We don't breed chihuahuas," said the kennel owner. "But we happen to have one that I got for arranging a mating between a male chihuahua from Paragould and a female chihuahua from Walnut Ridge. So you sure are welcome to swap," he said, reaching out for Friendly.

"Wait!" I said. "A person has got to say good-bye, don't they?" I looked into Friendly's eyes and wondered how I could make him understand. "I never wanted to get rid of you, Friendly. I only wanted to get rid of the aller—*Her-her-choo!*—of the allergy."

He licked my ear almost as if to tell me not to worry because any dog as friendly as Friendly would get along just fine.

Again Mr. Grant reached out, only this time I gave him my Friendly. As he took him away, I heard him say, "Rest of the collies going to be mighty happy to see you again."

When he returned, Friendly wasn't with him. "An allergy sure is a bothersome thing," said Mr. Grant. "Reason I know that is because I've had an allergy ever since I was about your age."

It was so hard to believe. "You got yourself an allergy to collies too?" I asked.

"Nope." Mr. Grant pointed to the bend in his suntanned arm. "Tomatoes—that's what gets my allergy going. One tomato and my arm breaks out like a strawberry patch."

"Tomatoes don't bother me a bit," I said proudly.

"Reckon that's what an allergy is," said Mr. Grant. "It's what don't bother some folks, bothers other folks a whole lot."

When we stopped in front of the chihuahua's run, a tiny fellow came rushing to the gate, barking. "That's the dog for me," I said.

On the drive back home I held the chihuahua in my lap while my folks went back to trying to pick out a baby name. I was hoping they'd find a better name for the baby than they found for me.

When Pa turned off the highway onto the dirt road leading to our farm, the puppy jumped off my lap. He stood on his toes, pressing his nose against the truck's window. I hollered, "Looky there! Look at Tippietoes!"

"Ohhhh," said Ma, turning her head. "Now ain't that something? And what a fine name for him too."

I put my hands against the little dog's cheeks and gave him a kiss between the eyes. "I now name you—*ah-ah*—— I now name you——*ah-ah-ah-choo!*"

"Oh *no!*" said Ma and Pa at exactly the same time.

But finally I was able to say, and say proudly, "I now name you Tippietoes."

By the time I crawled into bed, my eyes were red and itchy. My nose was sneezy and my chest was wheezy. Ma stood at my doorway. "Tippietoes going to sleep next to the cookstove tonight, but tomorrow evening we're going to take him back."

I shook my head no. "Mama, don't say that. I don't care nothing about no little allergy, cross my heart I don't. All I care about is my little dog. My own little Tippietoes."

"Girl, you ain't talking nothing but a heap of foolishness. I ain't about to let you walk around sick. Not as long as I'm your mama, 'cause I ain't that kind of mama. Now you get yourself to sleep."

At first recess, I told Miss Johnson about having an allergy, not just to long-haired dogs but to short-haired ones too.

"Maybe I can find still another secret in that book," she

said, bringing down the big book again. She fingered through a lot of pages before she finally began to read aloud: "People who have an allergy to both long-haired and short-haired dogs might not have an allergy to poodles, as they are the only dogs that never shed hair."

Pa explained to Mr. Grant what I had learned from the book. "So we'll be much obliged if you'll kindly swap Tippietoes here for one of your poodles."

"Fine with me," said Mr. Grant, reaching for Tippietoes.

"*Wait!*" I said, holding onto the little one for another moment. "A person still has to say good-bye." I patted his chin. He licked my fingers. "Good-bye, little boy, little Tippietoes. I'm sorry you couldn't be my dog."

I closed my eyes as I gave him over to Mr. Grant, who took him away. When he came back he said, "Come along folks. Let me introduce you to my poodles."

We followed him until he stopped at the gate of a chain-link fence. "Poodles may be just the right dog for a girl with an allergy," he said, pointing to two white dogs that looked more like fluffy powder puffs than real dogs. "Because they never have dandruff or a doggy odor. And the book is right. They never shed a single hair."

He unhooked the gate and I walked in saying, "This time I'm going to be lucky. This time I *hope* I'm going to be lucky."

"Hope so," said Ma and Pa at exactly the same moment.

Both poodles walked over to say hello. They were quite polite. I bent down and one of the puppies came closer. "Is it you?" I asked him.

He took one step closer, resting his fluffy little head in my hand. I whispered, "I'm going to take real good care of you."

Inside the crowded cab of the pickup truck, I held the poodle puppy on my lap as Pa turned on the headlights and started for home. My patting must have relaxed the little dog 'cause he closed his eyes and went to sleep.

After a while Ma said, "I think we ought to name the baby after my great-aunt Alberta."

Pa's nose crinkled. "What you want to name our baby after her for?"

Ma's nose climbed. "Ain't she my grandma's sister? The oldest living member of my family?"

"That nosy old lady!" said Pa.

"Aunt Alberta ain't one bit nosy," Ma corrected. "What she is, is interested. I'm disappointed in you, Mr. Eugene Lam—"

"Have you all noticed," I asked, hoping that my interruption would stop an argument from starting, "that I haven't sneezed even one time?"

Ma smiled. "Ain't it the truth."

"And Puffy will never have to go back to Mr. Grant's," I said.

"Puffy?" asked Pa, surprised.

"Don't you see," I asked, "how he's all puffy like cotton candy?"

Ma turned to look at Pa. "Beth has thought up three good names for three dogs while we is still fussing over one name for one baby."

Puffy opened his eyes and looked around. "You're here, Puffy," I said, putting my face into his white fluffiness. "And you're always going to be . . . my . . . my——*choo!* My——*ahhhhhhh—ey!*"

"Lord, don't go telling me I heard what I think I heard," said Ma, fixing her eyes on the ceiling of the truck.

"It ain't what you think," I said quickly. "I really—*ahhh-choo! Ah-choo-who!* I really think I'm catching Billy Boy Williams's cold. He had one at school today. Sneezed all over the place——choo, choo, choo, like that! Spreading his germs about."

Pa drove the truck over to the side of the road and turned off the engine. "Beth, I is sorry to disappoint you. I know how much you wanted a pup, but there ain't nothing I can do."

"If you take him back," I warned, "I ain't never going to live home again. For the rest of my life I'm going to live in the kennel with Puffy."

My mama patted my hand. "In this life you got to be happy about the good things and brave about the bad ones."

"I don't want to be brave," I shouted. "All I want is my little dog."

Pa started up the truck, made a U-turn on the highway, and headed back toward the kennel. "Ain't nothing in this wide world we can do," he said, shaking his head.

The next morning I asked Miss Johnson to bring down the book again. But after a while we stopped reading. It didn't have any more secrets to tell. I walked away 'cause I didn't have a single word for a single solitary soul. But later in the afternoon I told her, "I guess it's nobody's fault. But I reckon I'm learning to be brave about things I don't like."

"And I want you to know," said Miss Johnson, taking off her glasses, "that I think you're learning very well."

When the school bus stopped in front of our sign, I jumped off and with a running leap crossed the ditch.

"How come you shortcutting through the field again?" called Philip Hall. "Ain't no dog waiting for you today."

"Guess I know that," I said, wondering how I could have forgotten. And yet for some reason I really was in a hurry to get home.

When I reached the rise, I could see the chocolate-brown outline of my mother. But it didn't look like her, not exactly. After I passed the vegetable garden, I could see that it wasn't her. It was . . . my grandmother.

I started running my fast run. "Grandma, Grandma! Hello!"

"Howdy there, Beth babe," she called back.

I ran into her arms as she closed them around me. "How

come you're here? All the way from Walnut Ridge?"

Grandma smiled. "I came to see my new grandbaby. Born this very morning, a few minutes after nine."

"Where are they?" I asked.

"Shhhhh," she said, pointing to the inside of the house. "They are both real fine, but they're resting just now."

I asked, "Is it a . . . is it a brother?"

"A brother for you; a grandson for me," she said, hugging me some more.

I danced a circle around her. "My own little brother. He's going to be fun to take care of and fun to play with. Sometimes boys are almost as much fun to play with as girls. I've noticed that."

"Reckon I've noticed that too," said Grandma, joining my dance.

"What's my brother's name?"

Grandma stopped dancing. "Your folks ain't come to no decision on that," she said.

"Don't fret about that," I told her. "I happen to be good at names."

Then I heard Pa calling from inside the house, "Beth, come on in and meet up with your brother."

I closed the screen door quietly behind me the way I always remember to do when there is a visitor in the house. Pa stood at the door of his and Ma's bedroom and waved me on. "I want you to see something real pretty," he said.

Ma was sitting up in bed, propped up by two pillows. She was wearing her "sick" nightgown—the pink one with the lace running around the neck and collar. When I used to remind her that she ought to get some wear out of it 'cause she's never been sick a day in her life, Ma always said, "We'll see."

As I came closer, I saw something in her arms that I had never seen there before. A baby.

Ma said, "Fold your arms."

"Like this?" I asked.

"Just like that," she said, placing my soft little brother in my arms.

"Ohhhhh," I said, touching my lips to his warm head. "You are a beautiful baby brother. Baby brother Benjamin."

"Benjamin?" asked Ma. "Benjamin? *Benjamin!*—Oh, Lordy, yes. That's it. That's the name!"

Pa smiled. "Benjamin is a good strong name for a boy."

"Finally," said Grandma, coming into the room. "A name for the baby."

I put my face next to Baby Benjamin's and breathed in deep. I didn't sneeze. "You're always going to be our Baby Benjamin," I whispered in his ear. "And anyway, Mr. Grant wouldn't know what to do with a real baby."

The
Elizabeth Lorraine Lambert
& Friend Veg. Stand

April-June

If I'm the number-one best student now, it's because of what Doc Brenner told me, and I don't mean what he said about my outgrowing my allergies either. I'm talking about when he patted my wrist and told Ma and Pa, "Whole town is proud of this youngun."

He went on to tell us about this "smart young fellow" who went through four years of agricultural school with some assistance from him and his friends. Then he said that I had "undeniable talent" and when I was ready for college, he'd be pleased to help me get there too.

The doctor thought they could come up with at least half the money if Pa could manage the other half.

Fancy Annie brought Baby Benjamin out on the porch, sat down next to me, and, without so much as I beg your pardon, interrupted my thoughts. As I played with his two-month-old nibbly toes, I told her, "I've decided to become Randolph County's first veterinarian."

"Miss Elinor Linwood already done beat you to it," said Anne. " 'Cause she hasn't had a piece of meat in her mouth since that time she got a hunk of pot roast lodged in her throat."

I sighed. Being smart can sometimes be a burden. "Folks who don't eat meat are called vegetarians. I'm going to study in college to become an animal doctor—a *veterinarian*."

Anne got up and I followed her into the kitchen, where Ma was standing over the cookstove. Anne spoke to her back. "Would you listen to your younger daughter! Being a farmer's wife or even a teacher ain't good enough for our Beth. No sir! She's got to be more special than that. She's going to go to college to become a *vegernarian!*"

"Veterinarian," I corrected.

"Ain't nothing wrong with ambition," said Ma, placing a cover over the cast-iron skillet. "The Lord Jesus had it aplenty."

After supper I overheard Ma talking proud about what I had decided to become. Pa remarked that half of a heap of money is still a heap of money, "And I don't know no way to earn that kind of money."

For days after that I asked everybody I knew how to go about earning college money. My own teacher said right off that it's easier to earn money if you "first acquire a good education." When I told her that I needed the money first so I could become educated with it second, Miss Johnson was silent for a spell before replying, "That would make it considerably more difficult."

When days went by without a single money-making idea worth thinking about, I began to get more and more discouraged. It was Anne, of all people, who began encouraging me. "For a long time now," she said, "folks been getting me madder than a wet hen saying when the good Lord was passing out brains that little Beth stayed around long enough to get an extra helping. Well, is you going to prove all those folks wrong? Don't reckon you is."

"Well, those same people been making me just as mad," I admitted, "by telling me that you is the prettiest thing since the dawning of creation."

For a moment Anne and I stared at each other just as though we saw—or understood—something that we had never understood before. Together we drifted out on the front porch and sat down on the steps. We sat for a long spell, not saying anything, just watching the plow from Pa's tractor turning rows of limey green grass into rich chocolate earth.

Then I remembered something. On the cover of the very last issue of the *Saturday Evening Post* was a painting of a roadside vegetable stand, and crowding around to buy were some right fancy-looking folks from the city.

The next picture that I saw didn't come from remembering, 'cause what I was seeing had never yet been. Not as yet been. Philip Hall and I were selling vegetables from behind our own roadside stand. A sign read: THE ELIZABETH LORRAINE LAMBERT & FRIEND VEG. STAND.

When I told my sister what I was "seeing," she began beating my shoulder. "Oh, Beth baby, you've done done it again."

I jumped off the porch and started running to where Pa and his tractor were opening up the Arkansas earth. "Plant more!" I called to him in my loudest voice. "Plant more! Much *more!*"

For days and days after the planting I waited for the first green leaves to pop through the earth. First I worried that the seeds weren't going to sprout in such a dry soil. Then we had us some rain and I got to worrying that the moisture was sure to rot the roots. Even Ma noticed my concern, 'cause one day when she was helping me weed, she said that I was fretting more over my garden than Luther does over his "precious pigs."

Still, with all the work I put in, it wasn't until the first seedlings broke earth that I began to believe, really believe, that vegetables were going to grow and that those vegetables were going to make a veget—a veterinarian out of me.

After the seedlings appeared, we got what Pa said was "good growing weather," but that doesn't mean exactly what it sounds like it means. Since farmers are afraid to ever do even the tiniest bit of bragging—thinking that might change their luck for the worse—they say "bad" when what they really mean is "not bad." And when a farmer says "good growing weather," then that's his way of saying it couldn't be more perfect.

Well, the good growing weather brought forth worthy vegetables. Lovely tomatoes, crunchy corn, and watermelon sweeter than a candy bar.

And on the first free day of summer vacation Philip and I built a stand on the gravelly shoulder of the highway by placing some barn boards over a couple of rickety orange crates. When I began to nail on the sign that I had so carefully painted the night before, Philip read out loud: "The Elizabeth Lorraine Lambert & Friend Veg. Stand" in a voice so high that it actually cracked, probably from lack of oxygen. "That's not fair!"

I moved Philip's finger to the word *friend*. "See, I didn't leave you out."

He shook his head. "Not fair!"

"It is *too* fair," I insisted. "Whose idea was it? Who did the planting? The weeding? The picking? You is nothing but a Philip-come-lately."

THE ELIZABETH LORRAINE LAMBERT & Friend VEG. STAND

Philip only gave me a quick look that I couldn't quite read before going on about his business of arranging the tomatoes, watermelons, and corn in the shape of a pyramid on the counter.

"Sure does look nice," I said, hoping that a little appreciation would perk him right up. Philip's face flashed something that could be mistaken for a smile, and just when I was deciding whether or not to count that as progress. a dark blue car came to a stop in front of our stand. Our first customer! Now that was progress, sure enough.

The bald head that poked itself out the car window belonged to the bushy-eyed owner of the Busy Bee Bargain Store.

" 'Lo, Mr. Putterham," I called as he came over to look. "Want to buy some farm-fresh vegetables today?" When he didn't answer, I added, as a sort of extra attraction, ". . . At a bargain?"

Mr. Putterham seemed to take a fancy to one of the ears that was in dead center of Philip's pyramid. As he gave it a quick yank, it caused the great triangle of corn to level. Philip watched the destruction of his labor with obvious pain, but Mr. Putterham took no more notice of my partner's pain than he did of the great corn leveling. For one thing, he was too busy sniffing the corn, peeling down the shucks, and sniffing some more. Then he looked down at me just as though he had appointed himself the final judge at Judgment Day. "Thought you said you was selling *fresh* vegetables?"

"An hour ago that corn was still growing on its stalk."

When Mr. Putterham finally drove off, I was one dollar and ninety-five cents richer and a whole lot happier. Philip and I threw our arms around each other, jumped into the air, and made loud and joyful noises.

After the celebrating, I told Philip to mind the store while I made a trip back for more vegetables. Not only had Mr. Putterham bought every last ear of our corn, but he also bought the best two of our three watermelons.

At first I got to figuring that he probably bought that second melon to give a friend, but that was before I got to remembering what it is that folks in these parts say about Mr. Cyrus J. Putterham. "Old Putterham is so cheap he wouldn't give nobody nothing, not even a kind word."

I packed the cart, whose long-time missing wheel Luther had replaced as a going-in-business present to me, with a couple dozen ears of corn and two of our biggest melons. But I couldn't get over thinking how peculiar it is that some folks would pay out good money for the same vegetables that they could grow themselves.

As I pulled the rolling produce back along the dusty road, I could see up ahead that a car was parked near our stand. Another customer! I wanted to see him. Wanted to be there when he reached down into his pocket to bring out the money that was going to help pay my way through college.

Running when a person has to play steam engine to a cargo on wheels ain't the easiest thing to do. So while I couldn't exactly run, I did walk just as fast as I could. When I finally reached the highway, the car with a man and woman inside was just driving off.

I gave Philip Hall a congratulating pat on the back. "Reckon you must have sold them a good amount," I said, noticing that the last watermelon was now gone.

He shook his head no.

"What do you mean *no?*"

"What I means to say," said Philip pretending great patience, "is that they didn't buy nothing. And they didn't spend no money. Do you understand now what I mean when I say no?"

"No," I said. " 'Cause I don't see the watermelon. Who bought that?"

His head swirled to look at the place that was now made vacant by the missing melon. "Oh, that one," he said.

"Yep, that one. Who bought it?" I asked just at the moment I caught sight of some watermelon rinds (and only the rinds) lying in the gully. I didn't have to ask another question 'cause now I understood everything. "You good-for-nothing, low-down polecat of a Philip Hall! Those folks stopped to buy a melon, didn't they?"

He looked too surprised to answer so I just went on telling what I knew to be the truth. "But you didn't have a melon to sell, did you? Cause you already done ate it!"

Philip called me "crazy" and then he stopped talking. And if that wasn't bad enough, the cars too seemed to have stopped stopping. A couple of times, they slowed down and

I thought for sure they were going to stop, but they didn't. Don't know why, unless maybe they caught a look at Philip's sourer-than-a-lemon-ball face.

Another thing about this day that wouldn't stop was the sun. One of the real hot ones. I reckon I could've drunk a gallon of ice water. Reckon I could've even drunk a gallon of water without the ice.

Then I heard Philip's voice actually speaking. "We got us another customer. He pointed across the road to a red tow truck with the words WALNUT RIDGE GULF STATION neatly painted on its door.

After the baseball-capped garageman paid me for one melon and a half dozen ears of corn, I asked him if he knew my grandmother, Miz Regina Mae Forde. "She lives on Route 67 just north of Walnut Ridge."

"No," but he smiled a dimpled smile. "I'm going to be going right past her house to fetch a battery, so I can take you there and back if you've a mind to do some visiting."

I thought about the lemonade that Grandma makes with exactly the right number of sugar granules. I thought about the shade trees that circle her little house. And most of all I thought about Grandma.

I would have gone on thinking, but I was interrupted by my partner's voice. "Let's go, Beth. Please?"

As we walked up Grandma's now grassless path, I got a sudden thought. If she sees me so unexpectedly at her door, she'll right away think I'm bringing bad news.

Grandma has been a mite worried about us ever since Calvin Cook Senior was released from jail.

So I stayed hidden in the bushes while friend Philip walked up the front step and knocked hard against the wood door. After a moment's wait he knocked even harder. And when she didn't answer that one, I came out of hiding long enough to ask him to walk around back to see if she wasn't out hanging clothes. Well, he did, but she wasn't.

We sat on a piece of shady grass by the side of the road making bets on who would be coming along first: Grandma or the garageman. Just as I said, "Grandma," as though there wasn't room enough in this world for one speck of doubt, I saw the garageman's arm waving at us through the truck's open window.

About fifteen minutes later, when we came within viewing distance of our stand, I stabbed at the windshield. "What are those damn fool cows doing bunched around our stand?"

"They're our dairy cows," explained Philip as though that was the most natural explanation in the world. "Being brought back from the west pasture for milking."

The garageman hadn't come to a 100 percent complete stop before I was out of that truck flailing my arms as though they had been set into revolving sockets. "Shew! Shew, you dumb cows! Shew! Would you look what you've done to my business!"

All the cows moved leisurely on except one rust-and-white spotted Jersey, who took the only remaining ear of corn into her mouth without even bothering to see what my displeasure was about.

"You're dumb," I yelled at the Jersey. "Dumb, *dumb, dumb!*"

Then just as if to show me how she felt about my name-calling, she backed her perfectly enormous rump into the stand, sending all three melons to the ground. Two of them cracked, but the largest melon miraculously made the fall intact.

"*Dumb!*" I screamed, and the cow lifted her head as though to demonstrate her complete contempt at my shockingly bad behavior before sending her front foot through the last surviving melon. "Ohhh . . ." I said, feeling violent about the destruction of The Elizabeth Lorraine Lambert & Friend Veg. Stand.

"Her name's Eleanor," said Philip, with what sounded like pride. "She's one cow that always had a mind of her own."

I pointed my finger at him. "You and Eleanor are exactly alike! 'Cause neither of you got the sense God gave you!"

At the supper table I told Pa, Ma, Luther, and Anne about how my vegetable stand was destroyed when Philip Hall made me go with him to Walnut Ridge.

Pa put down his glass of buttermilk. "Show me your scars."

"My what?"

"Your scars," he said again. " 'Cause I never knowed nobody who could make my Beth do what she hadn't a mind to do, less'n of course, he beat you with a bull whip." Pa leaned his head back just like he always does when he lets go of a really fat laugh. "So show us your scars." He wasn't laughing alone either. They were all laughing their dang fool heads off. All excepting me.

I jumped up, slapping my hand down upon the oilcloth. "Reckon I should have knowed you folks would rather take sides with Philip Hall than with your own flesh and blood."

Ma gave my hand little taps saying, "Now, now, nobody in this world is taking sides against you."

Tears were coming on, coming on too strong for stopping. I ran into my room to throw myself across my bed. I cried as quietly as I could, wondering why I hadn't seen it before. How they all love Philip Hall better'n me. Well, let them! It don't make me no never mind.

After a while I had to quit crying 'cause it was giving me a headache and I was, truth to tell, plumb tired of lying across the bed. So I tiptoed out the front door so quietly that I didn't have to face a single solitary Lambert.

I passed Pa's garden of the good growing weather, admired the corn stalks which seemed to grow taller and prouder with each sunrise. And on each stalk, ears—lots of corn ripened ears, ready for the picking. Plenty there for a heap of selling. And in the next rows was the tomatoes that should be able to win a blue ribbon at anybody's country fair. But the bluest ribbon should be saved for the watermelon. The reddest, sweetest melons in all of Randolph County.

The sun was lowering, but there was still light enough on the rutty back road that I followed out to the highway. When I reached what remained of The Elizabeth Lorraine Lambert & Friend Veg. Stand, I surveyed the damage. The corn was muddied and bruised; mashed tomatoes littered the gravel shoulder, and the bursted watermelons had become a feast for ants and flies.

The boards and the crates were unbroken although the company sign did suffer from a muddy hoofprint directly across the word *Friend.*

As I replaced the boards across the crates I began thinking about what really happened. I thought about the God-given good growing weather, about Pa's extra planting, about Ma making the time to help me weed my garden. I thought about Luther's repairing the cart, Anne's encouragement, and, God help me, I even thought about Philip Hall who had always been better at talking than at working. And isn't that what I really wanted him for? For company?

Sweet Philip. Did he really force me to go to Walnut Ridge? Although I didn't come close to smiling, I did come closer to understanding what Pa and the rest of the family found funny.

I threw the feast-for-flies melons across the road into the

gully and swept away the tomatoes with a willow branch. Then with only one mighty swing with a roadside rock, I nailed the company sign back onto the stand.

As I stepped back to look it all over, I saw only one thing still needed doing. So with my hand I brushed away —carefully brushed away—the mud from the word *Friend*.

The Pretty Pennies picket

July

I no sooner set the ice-cold pitcher of lemonade on the porch when I saw the Blakes' green pickup truck stirring up the dust as it traveled down our rutty road. "Ma," I called through the screen door. "Bring out the cookies! The Pretty Pennies are a-coming."

Right away the door opened, but it wasn't Ma. It was Luther wearing a fresh white dress shirt and the blue pants from his Sunday suit. While Susan, Esther, and Bonnie jumped off the truck's back platform, Luther didn't hardly pay no never mind. It wasn't until Ginny the gorgeous climbed down that Luther, wearing a very pleasant expression, took a couple of giant steps toward her and asked, "How y'all getting along, Ginny?"

Ginny didn't get a chance to answer 'cause the one girl who folks say was born into this world talking answered my brother's question. "Fried to a frizzle," said Bonnie Blake. "And that lemonade yonder looks mighty refreshing."

After the lemonade was drunk and the cookies eaten, I performed my duties by rapping on the floor of the porch and saying, "This here meeting of the Pretty Pennies Girls Club is now called to order."

"Trouble with this club," said Bonnie without waiting until we got to new business, "is that we never do nothing but drink lemonade and talk about the boys in the Tiger Hunters' Club."

Heads bobbed up and down in agreement.

Bonnie smiled as though she was onto something big. "What this club needs is somebody with new ideas about things that are fun doing."

Then Ginny did something unusual. She found that one sliver of a moment which Bonnie wasn't cramming with words and said, "We just go from one meeting to the next meeting without ever doing anything. Reckon we could use a new president."

Even before Ginny's words were being applauded, I knew there was some truth to be found in them. We do just sit around gabbing—which is fun—but it was the same amount of fun before I got the idea that we had to become a club. "Philip Hall and the Tiger Hunters ain't the only ones can be a club!" And it was also me that told them how it was a known fact that clubs have more fun than friends. Suddenly I felt ashamed of myself for having promised more than I delivered, but mostly I felt angry with the Pretty Pennies, who were fixing to dump their president without as much as a "begging your pardon."

I looked up at the porch ceiling, looking for something like a good idea waiting to bore through my brain. Well, I looked, but I didn't see nothing but ceiling paint. So I closed my eyes and sure enough something came to me. I waved my hands for quiet. "It so happens that I do have a wonderful idea, but I was waiting to tell y'all about it."

Bonnie began, "Is it fun? 'Cause I got me plenty of chores to do at home so if it's—"

I broke right in. "Quiet! Now next month the Old Rugged Cross Church has their yearly picnic, and I've been thinking that we oughta challenge the Tiger Hunters to a relay race."

"Five of them," said Bonnie. "Five of us."

"Yes siree," I agreed. "But they is going to be something special about our five 'cause we're going to be wearing a special uniform which we ourselves made."

Right away I noticed how all the girls came alive when I mentioned the uniform, so I went on to describe it. "With the money we got in our club treasury, we're going to buy big T-shirts and some different-colored embroidery thread for each Pretty Penny. And then"—my finger traced a crescent across my chest—"we could all embroider the words: THE PRETTY PENNIES GIRLS CLUB OF POCAHONTAS, ARKANSAS." I said, really beginning to feel my presidential powers, "And if we were of a mind to, we could also embroider on the names of all the folks we like."

"You going to embroider on the name of Mister Phil Hall?" asked Bonnie in that cutesy-pooh voice of hers.

I laughed just as though I had nary a worry in this world. Oh, sometimes I think that Philip Hall still likes me, but at other times I think he stopped liking me the moment he stopped being the number-one best everything.

But he wouldn't do that, would he? Stop liking me just because I'm smarter than him? I can't help it and, anyway, Miss Johnson herself said that if I'm going to become a veterinarian I'm going to have to become the best student I know how to be.

On Saturday afternoon all us Pennies went into the Busy Bee Bargain Store for white T-shirts big enough to get lost in. After a lot of discussion, we dropped five T-shirts, fifty skeins of embroidery thread, five embroidery hoops, and five packages of needles onto the wrapping counter in front of Mr. Cyrus J. Putterham.

After taking our money, he pulled one tan sack from beneath the counter and began shoveling everything into it.

"Oh, no, sir," I corrected. "We each need our own bags."

His bushy eyebrows made jumpy little elevator rides up

and then down. "Don't you girlies have any feeling? Five sacks cost me five times as much as one."

"But we need them," I explained. " 'Cause we're not even related."

He pulled out four more. "Costs me money, each one does. But you wouldn't care nothing about that. Kids never do!"

As we Pretty Pennies embroidered our shirts on the following Wednesday evening, we drank Bonnie Blake's strawberry Kool-Aid, ate her potato chips, and gabbed on and on about those Tiger Hunters.

We even sent them a letter saying that they ought to get busy practicing their relay running 'cause we Pretty Pennies were aiming to beat them to pieces.

The next meeting was at Ginny's house, where we all sat in a circle on the linoleum floor and talked about our coming victory over the boys while we munched popcorn from a cast-iron skillet and embroidered away. Then from outside: *Bam . . . bam . . . bam-my . . . bam . . . bam!*

Our embroidery dropped to our laps as we grabbed onto one another. Bonnie pointed toward the outside while, for the first time in her life, her mouth opened and closed and closed and opened without a single sound coming out.

Finally, Esther, who almost never had a word to say, said, "Wha—What was that?"

"Let's see," I said, moving cautiously and pulling Esther along with me toward the door. I peeked out just in time to see two figures (both less than man size) race deeper into the halflight before disappearing from sight.

Bonnie, Ginny, and Susan were still sitting like frozen statues.

"It's OK," I told them. "Whoever they were—and I think I know who they were—have already ran away."

Esther followed me out on the porch, where there was a rock the size of a crow's nest and sticking to this rock was a sheet of wide-lined paper. I pulled off the paper, which had been stuck on with a wad of gum, and read aloud:

> Dear Pretty Pennies,
> You ain't pretty!
> You ain't pennies!
> And you ain't never going to beat us neither!
> > President Philip Hall
> > Bravest of all the brave Tiger Hunters
> > and Lt. Gordon Jennings (also Brave)
> P.S. Why wait for the church picnic to relay race? Meet us at the schoolyard on Saturday and we'll win!

Everybody was really mad and we all began talking at once about those Tiger Hunters who run around scaring the wits out of a person. Bonnie thought we ought to teach them a lesson. "Specially that Phil Hall."

I'd have liked nothing better, but probably for a different reason. It wasn't the scare so much as what he said about not being pretty that ruffled my feathers. Did he mean nobody was pretty? Or was nobody but me pretty? Or . . . or was everybody pretty excepting me? Next thing I knew I was shouting, "We're going to get those low-down polecats!" Then while I had everybody's attention, I gave them their final instructions: "Next Saturday we'll race. Finish embroidering on our club name, front and back. Then everybody wash your shirts so our club name will be clean easy reading. All the folks in Pocahontas is going to know just who it was that beat them Tiger Hunters."

The next morning Philip didn't show up for work at The Elizabeth Lorraine Lambert & Friend Veg. Stand. Well, he's probably just mad or practicing up his relay running. Or maybe Mr. Hall has him doing chores. But that's the unlikeliest explanation of them all.

Without him there ain't no games or giggles, but today there's not a speck of boredom either 'cause I'm just too busy embroidering my T-shirt and running my business. And with every sale my college money grows. I'm going to become a veterinarian yet.

It was just before bedtime on Friday night that I stitched the last beautiful stitch on my shirt. I held it out for better viewing. Even with the soil from two weeks of handling along with Baby Benjamin's mashed-in, smashed-in sweet potato, it was beautiful. Just beautiful!

As I began to draw the wash water, Ma told me to get to bed 'cause I'd be needing my strength for the big race tomorrow. She took the shirt from my hand as she gave me a light shove toward the bedroom. "Reckon I can do the washing if you can do the resting."

When the morning sky came again to Pocahontas, I woke wide awake just as though I hadn't been sleeping at all but only resting up before the big race.

At the kitchen table Ma sat in front of a bowl of peas needing shelling, but her hands sat unmoving in her lap. I tried to remember the last time I had seen my mother just sitting without actually doing anything. All I said was "Morning, Ma," but it was enough to make her look as though she was staring at a spook.

"Reckon I'm going to have to tell you," she said, holding tight to the bowl. "But I don't know how to tell you . . . It's about your shirt. Done shrunk to midget size. Sure did."

As Pa drove down Pocahontas's Main Street, I spotted the rest of the Pennies leaning up against a yellow fireplug. A block away Pa turned his car and angle-parked in front of the E-Z Cash & Carry Market. When the Pennies saw me walking toward them, they all shook their heads just like I was doing something wrong. What does that mean? That I'm not wearing my uniform? No, but I'm carrying it wrapped like a fish in an old newspaper to show them what they'd never believe without seeing. Anyway, they're not wearing theirs either. Too lazy to finish their embroidery probably.

Bonnie began by saying that it was an ordinary washing

powder, one of those kinds that they're always talking about over the radio. Then Esther, who would never interrupt anybody, interrupted to say that her water was barely warm.

I was losing patience with everybody talking, everybody understanding but me. "What are you all babbling about mild soap and barely warm water for?"

Suddenly Ginny whipped from a grocery bag a white T-shirt so shrunk that the embroidery's lettering was no longer readable. "We is talking about this."

First we talked about our wasted efforts and then we talked about our wasted money and then we talked about what nobody could understand: what caused the shrinkage.

"Listen here," I said suddenly. "We bought something in good and honest faith that didn't turn out to be a bit of good. Well, if we all go down to the Busy Bee and explain the situation to Mr. Putterham, then he'll give us back our money. Probably even apologize that he can't pay us for our trouble."

"What Mr. Putterham is you talking about?" asked Bonnie, cocking her head like a trained spaniel. "The only Mr. Putterham I know wouldn't apologize to his ma if he ran her down in the broad daylight."

I told her right off. "Trouble with you, Miss Bonnie, is that you ain't got no faith in human nature."

Still, the thought that old bushy eyes ever had a mother was surprising. Reckon I just couldn't see Mr. Putterham having anything that couldn't turn a profit.

Even though I walked into the Busy Bee as slow as I could possibly walk, the others carefully managed to walk even slower. They stayed behind me, pushing me on toward the wrapping counter and the awesome presence of Cyrus J. Putterham. As I watched him tying a piece of string around a shoe box, I got to wishing that one of the other girls had replaced me as president of the Pennies; then they'd be standing here on the firing line instead of me.

The merchant lifted his eyebrows at me, which was a kind of a cheapskate way of asking what I wanted without actually bothering to ask.

"Well, uh . . . Mr. Putterpam—ham! Mr. Putterham, it's uh . . . about what happened two Saturdays ago when we all bought T-shirts from your store. We washed them like we wash anything else," I said, removing the newspaper from my shirt to hold it up. "And they all five shrunk up like this."

He stretched his lips into a hard straight line. "How much you pay for that shirt?"

"Eighty-nine cents."

"See?"

What did he want me to see? "Sir?"

A short blast of air rushed through his nostrils and I came to understand that his patience zipped off on that blast of air. "Something you girls paid only eighty-nine cents for isn't going to last forever. Why, eighty-nine cents for a T-shirt is mighty cheap."

"Oh, no, sir," I corrected him. "Paying eighty-nine cents for something that ain't never been worn is mighty expensive."

He waved his hand as though he was shooing a fly. "All right, I was nice enough to listen to you girls and now y'all get on out of here. I got me a store to run."

"Yes, sir," I said pleasantly. "We appreciate your attention, sure do. But what we really want is for you to refund us our money 'cause a shirt that ain't fit to be washed ain't fit to be sold."

"Get on out of here!" Both his hands went flapping in the air. "Now get!"

We may have left the store like scared chicks, but once outside we became more like mad wet hens. Esther kept saying, "Imagine!" Or sometimes she'd vary it with "Would you imagine that!"

Then, as if we didn't have enough trouble, the Tiger Hunters led by the bravest of all the brave Tiger Hunters came up to say that we were going to be beaten so bad that it would be a long time before we showed our face in Pocahontas again.

"Don't fret about it," I told him. " 'Cause I don't think I want to show my face anymore, anyway." A warm tear had begun to worm its way down my cheek.

Philip looked uncomfortable. What's the matter? Hadn't he ever seen a tear before? "We don't have to relay race today," he was saying. "We can put it off until the Sunday of the Old Rugged Cross Church picnic."

We shook hands on it, but I was not able to say any more. Talking took too much effort. So Bonnie explained while Ginny showed Philip and his Tiger Hunters what happened to our shirts. Right away Philip said, "We don't have to let Mr. Putterham get away with that. That's robbery!"

Philip's comment about its being a robbery struck me like one of God's own revelations!

At the far end of Main Street, sitting on a square of grass, is the old red brick courthouse where Sheriff Nathan Miller has a narrow office and two barred cells. As the Pennies and Hunters strode up the courthouse walk, old men sitting out on sunny park benches looked up.

The sheriff told us all to crowd on in. "I'll never forget what good police work you and Phil did in capturing those fowl thieves. You know, no farmer has reported any livestock missing since they left town."

His words encouraged me to tell him about our "robbery" at the hands of the merchant Putterham. I watched the sheriff's face grow more and more thoughtful. Finally he said, "I'm sorry, but there ain't no way I can help you out."

". . . But why?"

With his booted feet, the sheriff pushed his chair from his desk. "Follow me," he said, already walking with strong strides from his office.

Outside, the men on the benches now seemed doubly

surprised to see us kids half-running in order to keep up with Randolph County's long-legged lawman. A block down Main Street and then two blocks down School Street to the last house at the end of the block. The sheriff walked up the driveway and into the backyard. At a backyard sand-pile a little boy dressed in diapers and pullover shirt tod-dled over, saying, "Dadadadada."

The sheriff picked him up and then asked me, "What do you think of my boy's shirt?"

Surely eleven folks didn't walk all the way over here just to look at a tight-fitting baby shirt. It seemed silly, but he really did want my opinion. "I reckon it's a nice enough baby shirt," I told him.

"Uh-hun!" answered the more than six feet of sheriff as though he had suddenly struck gold. "Uh-hun," he re-peated. "For a baby shirt it's mighty fine, but it wasn't bought to be no baby's shirt. No Sir! It was bought for me. Last Saturday I paid eighty-nine cents for that T-shirt at the Busy Bee Bargain Store."

"You too!!—Then why don't you—"

"Because selling bad merchandise," he said, "can get a merchant in trouble with his customers without getting him in trouble with the law."

We Pretty Pennies walked with the Tiger Hunters back toward Main Street like a bunch of beaten soldiers. No rea-son for hurrying. No good left in the day nohow. Then it struck me like a pie in the face. Why are we defeated? Ten of us and only one of them Putterhams. "Stop!" I said, whirling around like a general of the army. "We ain't giving up this battle!"

"We ain't?" asked Philip.

I was the fightingest president the Pretty Pennies would ever have. "No, we ain't, 'cause if we all stood out in front of the Busy Bee Bargain Store showing off our shrunken shirts, then old Mr. Putterham would be so embarrassed he'd have to refund our money."

I broke into a run, followed by Philip Hall, followed by the rest of them. In front of the Busy Bee, we all formed a loose line—a Penny, a Hunter, a Penny, and so forth. "Pretty Pennies and Tiger Hunters. When we're working together we'll call ourselves the great Penny Hunters," I said.

Since Philip Hall didn't look exactly thrilled by my suggestion, I said, "Well, would you rather be called the Pretty Tigers?" His groan gave me his answer.

When a heavy woman with three chilluns slowly made her way toward the Busy Bee door, Bonnie approached her. A moment later she was spreading out her doll-size shirt across her chest while the woman shook her head and said, "I'm going to do my trading at Logan's."

The very next person who was persuaded not to spend money at the Busy Bee was my sister, Anne. She said she could buy fingernail polish at the dime store just as well.

After Anne, there was our preacher, the Reverend Ross,

who was going to buy some white handkerchiefs from Putterham, but the Reverend said he'd "be happy to respect your picket line."

"Respect our what?" I asked.

"Folks who is standing like some of God's own soldiers against the world's injustices is," said the Reverend Ross, "a picket line."

Never before in my whole life had I ever felt so important, but then never before had I been on special assignment for God.

Just then a family of five reached for the Busy Bee's door and I called out, "Don't you folks go buying things in there unless"—I held up my shirt—"you don't object to shrinking."

"Lordy," said the wife, coming right over to get a closer look. "Now ain't that a pity?"

Mr. Putterham stepped outside the door. "What's this? What's going on here?"

I turned to watch Philip Hall 'cause I didn't want to miss seeing him speak right up to that old man merchant. But the only thing I saw was the bravest Tiger Hunter of them all with his mouth flung open, looking for all the world like he would never again be able to speak.

The proprietor's eyes now swept past Philip and were looking down the long picket line. "Don't tell me that all you kids have been struck speechless? Somebody better tell me what's going on!"

I took one step forward. "I reckon you oughta know that we is picketing your store, Mr. Putterdam—ham! Mr. Putterham."

His big, bushy eyebrows jumped up and down as though they were skipping rope. "You is doing WHAT? And to WHOM?"

"We is"—my mouth felt too dry for stamp licking—"picketing you," I said, grateful that the words actually sounded.

"Now you listen here, you," he said. "Nobody pickets Cyrus J. Putterham, Pocahontas's leading merchant. Know that?"

"Yes, sir."

"Good," he said, smiling a pretend smile. "Then y'all get on out of here."

"Uh . . . no, sir," I said, trying to remember the Reverend Ross's words about being one of God's own soldiers.

"What do you mean No, sir?" he asked, allowing his voice to rise into a full shout. "You just got through saying Yes, sir."

"Uh, well, sir, that was my answer to your question."

Mr. Putterham blinked as though my words were being spoken in a strange new language. I tried again. "What I was saying, Mr. Putterjam . . . ham! Mr. Putterham, was yes, sir, I know all about you being Pocahontas's leading merchant. But no, sir, we ain't moving from our picket line. Not until we get our money back."

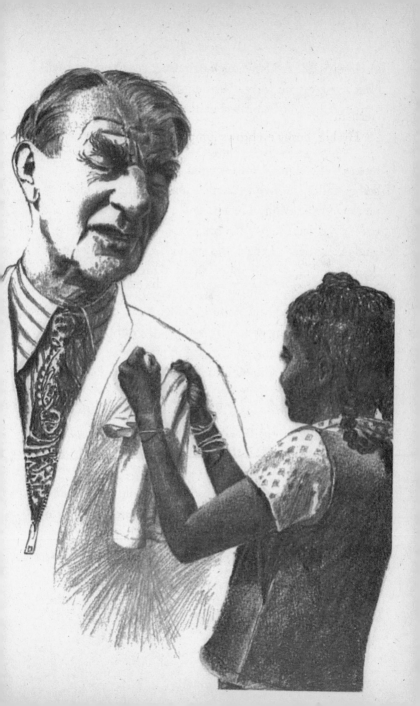

His eyes told me how much he wanted me to understand. "But if I give you folks your money back, then everybody who ever bought bad merchandise from me will be wanting their money back too."

From the picket line a single voice called, "Give back the money!" Then more voices, more Pennies and Hunters together calling, "Give back the money!" And I joined my voice with the Penny Hunters and even some folks on the street who were now chanting, *"Give back the money!"* And taken together the voices sounded as though they were doing a lot more demanding than asking.

The shopkeeper threw up his hands. "All right, all right." He smiled, but it wasn't what you'd call a sincere smile. "Making my customers happy is the only thing that's ever been important to Cyrus J. Putterham. Take your shirts back to the wrapping counter for a full and courteous refund."

After all the shirt money was safely back in the hands of our treasurer, Bonnie Blake, I spoke again to the merchant. "There is one more thing, Mr. Putterpam—ham! Mr. Putterham."

"As long as you girls are satisfied—well, that's thanks enough for me. Why, my very business is built on a foundation of square and fair."

"Yes, sir," I agreed. "Would you mind giving us back our embroidery money?"

"Your what?"

I presented him with the cash register receipt. "Two dollars and fifty cents worth of embroidery thread, ruined when our shirts shrunk."

For a moment I thought his face was growing angry, but then he sighed and placed the additional two-fifty on the counter.

"Thanks, Mr. Putterham."

He smiled and this time it didn't look all that insincere. "You called me Putterham. Finally you did it right."

I smiled back at him. "And finally, Mr. Putterham, so did you."

The Old Rugged
Cross Church picnic

August

With a soft turkey underfeather, I traced the initials E. L. L. across my sister's motionless leg. When that didn't wake Anne, I ran the very tip of the feather in and out between her toes. Her toes squeezed backward and, for at least a moment, her mouth wiggled from side to side. Was she about to wake? She wasn't.

Wouldn't you think that a person would be up and raring to go on the Sunday of the Old Rugged Cross Church picnic? Wouldn't you think they'd bounce out of bed, knowing full well that the church bus ain't gonna wait?

Not even if that someone happens to be the prettiest thing since Salome? No, not even then. 'Cause the folks wouldn't want to wait and the driver wouldn't want to wait even though Jason Savage and Herbie Ferrell would.

Suddenly I threw back my hand and was just about to give Fancy Annie a slap on the behind when I thought better of it. She'd be so mad she'd change her mind about letting me wear her huaraches. What I needed was a way to wake her without her ever guessing that it was me. And I think . . . I think I just thought of a way.

In the top drawer of Pa's bureau was the flashlight whose beam was bright enough to make anybody think that they is sleeping face up under the noontime sun. I brought the light beam to the closed eyelids of my sleeping sister. For longer than a moment, nothing happened and then something did. Anne said, "Hhhhppah," before flopping over to face the wall.

And again I brought the light to her eyes—only closer. Much closer. A sliver of time passed and then a sliver bit more before Anne bolted upright crying like a frightened animal.

I hid the flashlight behind my back. "Well, ain't it nice, having Miss Anne among the woke?"

"I dreamt," she said as though relieved to be awake, "that Jason Savage and me were taking a walk. I told him, it's awfully hot . . . can't breathe . . . got to find shade. But there wasn't no shade. No tree, no house, no shade of no kind."

Sometimes even I don't like the things I do. "Oh, forget it," I told her. "Dreams don't mean a thing."

Her eyes narrowed as though they were still trying to keep out the sun. "But it was so real! No air for breathing and the sun all the time beating down on us!"

I tried changing the subject. "Know what today is?" She didn't answer, only stared at me through shaded eyes. "Today is relay race day," I said. "The Sunday of the Old Rugged Cross Church picnic! And if we all ain't out on that highway by eight o'clock, that bus going to go tooting on off without us."

"You and the rest of the family go on ahead," she said, falling back against her pillow. "Don't reckon I feel like no picnic today."

"You didn't have no bad dream," I admitted, bringing forth the flashlight. "This was the sun," I said, clicking on the flashlight, "that you couldn't get away from."

"You!" she said, looking first at me and then at the light beam.

"Well, you sure wasn't waking by yourself! The bus ain't a-gonna wait. And if I had given you just one hit across your bottom, then you'd of been so mad that you wouldn't have let me borrow your huaraches."

After moments of squinting at me in anger, she reached under her bed, pulled out her made-in-Mexico sandals, and dropped them at my feet, saying, "Don't you ever do that again! Heah?"

I gave little bobs of my head while examining the floorboards. Anne must have understood that my nods were really an apology because she picked up her towel and went off to wash without another word.

At exactly thirty minutes before the hour of eight, her most royal and fancy highness, Miss Anne Lambert, took a long look into the mirror before announcing, "I'm ready to go a-picnicking." Mama picked up the blanket which a little later on was going to be ate off of, rested on, and probably even snoozed upon. Pa carried a shopping bag full of fried turkey and egg-salad (but not chicken egg) sandwiches, cornbread, popcorn, and oranges.

Luther, wearing his battered blue baseball cap and his catcher's mitt, was the first of the Lambert six out the door, followed by Ma, Pa, and Anne beneath a flowery bonnet. While I proudly wore my new bought-at-Logan's and just-embroidered Pretty Penny T-shirt and carried Baby Benjamin, who wasn't wearing nothing more (or less) than a pair of diapers.

The walk down the dusty road to the highway is, according to my pa's calculations, a five-minute walk in January and a fifteen-minute walk in August. Well, this August morning we must have made the walk in January time, 'cause nobody was taking any chances on missing that bus.

Already waiting at the gravelly highway's edge was enough people for a small picnic. First of all there was Philip Hall and his folks, Mr. and Mrs. Moses Hall, and his big brothers, Jeb, Leon, and Eugene, with their wives and chilluns.

Just as soon as I asked Philip if the Tiger Hunters were ready for racing, Baby Benjamin burped up some sour-smelling milk against the shoulder of my Pretty Penny T-shirt.

"When you going to be old enough to stop that?" I asked, while applying my hand and some fresh spit to the shoulder smell. He's almost six months old now and outside of eating and being carried around by me, there ain't nothing he seems to enjoy so much as a good burp.

I looked down the road to see the lipstick-red bus which belonged to the Old Rugged Cross Church coming down the road as though it had to make time. Even before the old thing came to a complete stop, every window had a head, or sometimes two, popping out and calling "Howdy!" As soon as the door opened, the Reverend Ross jumped off to welcome everybody on board. Wearing a short-sleeve sport shirt with printed-on palm trees, instead of his usual preacher's collar, made him look for all the world like an ordinary man. He shook hands with everybody who boarded, saying, "Climb on board, Brother. Climb on board, Sister, and climb on board, little children."

The Pretty Pennies, who were all wearing brand-new and just-embroidered T-shirts, whistled and waved me to the back, the very back, where they had "captured" the only seat that ran the width of the bus.

Two rows in front of us Philip slid into a seat saved for him by the Tiger Hunters. Gordon poked Philip with his elbow and said, "Tell those Not-so-Pretty Pennies how we're going to beat them in the relay races. Beat them to Kingdom Come!"

At that, Bonnie Blake gave me a poke to my ribs, saying, "And you tell them Kitty Catchers that they couldn't beat an egg, not even iffen their breakfast depended upon it."

"Oh, yeah?" said Gordon.

"Oh, yeah!" answered Bonnie.

I didn't take no special notice of Bonnie and Gordon's argument until I heard Philip Hall say, "Don't let that silly girl get your goat. Don't you know there ain't no girl alive can run as fast as no boy? And that's the Lord's truth!"

Suddenly I was out of my seat, pointing an angry finger at him. "You take that back!"

"Will not!"

"Last chance," I warned.

His lower lip pushed forward. "Ain't taking nothing you is offering," said Philip Hall. "Not even your last chances."

"Bet you our Pretty Penny shirts that we'll win."

"OK," he said, smiling as though he was putting something over on us. "We'll bet you your shirts."

"But you can only get our shirts if the Tiger Hunters win," I said. "But iffen the Pretty Pennies win then the Tiger Hunters will have to become our personal slaves for a whole week."

"Deal!" cried Philip, putting his hand out in a war shake that would make our bet as real and as true as if it had been signed in blood in front of a hundred judges.

"Jesus is a-listening," sang out the lone voice of the Reverend Ross before the passengers joined with him on the second line, "Don't make a sound . . . Oh, Jesus is a-listening . . . Don't make a sound."

And everybody was happy and singing away. The only exception (if I was of a mind to notice) was them Tiger Hunters, who were too busy messing around to do much singing. Philip was hanging onto an iron luggage rack high over the seat.

I warned him. "Better get down from there before somebody mistakes you for a chimpanzee and ships you off to the Little Rock Zoo."

He let go of one hand to strike himself across the chest. "I'm the Great Phil, King of the Mountain."

Past Imboden the land grew beautiful with watermelon-shaped lakes and popcorn clouds. The smell was of pine and mountain laurel and I couldn't see no place that wouldn't make a fine place for a picnic. At the sign, HARDY, ARK. — POP. 692, the bus slowed and some clapping broke out.

The picnic grounds at Hardy was a soft green valley between two mountains with a narrow but fast-moving river running through. The Tiger Hunters raced to the edge, pulling off shoes, throwing off shirts to touch the tippy-most points of their toes to the water with all the courage of a turkey in a thunderstorm.

"Careful," I called to Philip, while walking right into the water. "You might get your little toesies wet."

The look he threw me was anything but friendly. "I'm King Phil, King of that mountain," he said, pointing to its peak. "And if I've a mind to, I'll push you off."

"You're no more King of the Mountain than you are Man in the Moon."

Then Philip reached to the bank to pick up one of my borrowed huaraches. "Whose pretty sandal is this?" he asked as though he didn't want nothing more in this world but to find the owner so as to return it. Polite like.

"It is mine so would you kindly put it right back where you got it."

He held out the shoe toward me as he stepped closer. "Oh," he said sweetly, "I didn't know it belonged to you, little Beth."

"Well, it does," I said, reaching out to take it.

Suddenly he whirled the tan shoe across the river, shouting, "Catch, Gordy. Catch!"

I cried out as Anne's prize headed toward open water. My eyes closed; it was too painful to watch. But a moment later I opened them to a miracle. Gordon had actually saved Anne's huarache from a drowning.

Gordon was smiling like he had found a really new game. "Here," he said, holding out the shoe temptingly. "Take it if you want it."

It didn't take one bit of smartness to know what that

low-down polecat was up to. Only one step toward him and he'd have that shoe flying off toward Philip, Bobby, Jordan or Joshua.

I had to make him listen. "Gordon, don't throw it! Please! That's Anne's shoe and water ain't good for sandals that come all the way from Mexico."

"Want this?" he asked, holding it almost within my reach. "Then come and get it."

Thinks he can goad me into reaching for it so he could throw it Lord-knows-where. What if I made a really quick lunge? Reckon I could get . . . No, reckon not! My only chance is in talking him out of the game. "If something happens to that huarache, my sister wouldn't ever talk to me again. Please. Oh, please don't throw it!"

Again Gordon smiled as though he was on speaking terms with the devil himself as he repeated, "You want this? Then come and—"

Suddenly the huarache was jerked out of his hand by Philip Hall. "That shoe oughtna get wet. Didn't you hear Beth explain it to you?"

Under a shade tree Mama had spread out the blanket and set the food on top. Every family had pretty much the same idea because the picnic area was abloom with colorful chenille bedspreads, white sheets, and patchwork quilts. After all the folks had about finished eating their home-brought food and drinking their soda water, the Reverend went around distributing ice-cream cups.

Bonnie and Gordon almost missed out on the ice cream because they were too much into their fussing over whether the Pretty Pennies or the Tiger Hunters were going to win the relay races. Too bad, because I for one had been hoping that everybody would forget all about that. If we just happened to lose and the Pennies had to give up their shirts— why, they'd never forgive me.

With a branch Gordon drew a line in the dirt. "We can start the race here and run it in five relays, down to the river and back."

I always knew that Philip Hall was taller than all of us Pretty Pennies, but for the first time I noticed that Gordon was too. Taller with longer legs, and longer legs are faster. Always?

I told him, "You can't go around making up racing rules. You ain't the president of the Tiger Hunters, know that?"

Gordon must have believed in the wisdom of my words 'cause he went off down toward the river to fetch Philip while I went to lie down on our blanket and think. I think too much as it is. If I ever get us Pennies out of this mess, I'm going to glue a stop light on the tip of my tongue. Least thataways I'll have a red light telling me to stop my mouth before it goes roaring off into trouble.

I glanced around to see if anybody else felt miserable. But if they did they sure didn't show it. My pa was reading Mr. Moses Hall the letter he received from *Turkey World* magazine.

Dear Mr. Lambert:

*I apologize for taking all these months to re-
spond to your letter, but I couldn't decide from
which species of animal came your turkey thief.*

*However, after much consideration and even
further deliberation, I have now concluded that
the thief could only come from the species*
Homo sapiens. *Man!*

> *Sincerely yours,*
> *Thomas J. McCabe*
> *(The Answer Man)*

Gordon politely waited until Pa finished reading to com-
plain to Mr. Hall how the Tiger Hunters can't race without their president. "And he's nowhere in sight."

"You mean he ain't with you either?" asked the dairy-
man. "When he didn't join up with the rest of us Halls for
the eats, I just figgered he was munching on somebody
else's baloney."

"No, sir," answered Gordon. "I haven't seen Phil since
he was fooling around near the river."

At that, Philip's pa looked at my pa, and then they both
jumped to their feet and took off toward the water. And so
did I. Where was he? When I couldn't find him there, I
looked up to the sky. "Oh, please, God, let him be found
safe and sound." My eyes ran across the green pine
mountains. "You can bring Philip back safe, God. You're

King of the Universe. King of the Mountains." King of the Mountain? Where had I heard that before? From Philip Hall, that's who!

With his clothes on, Mr. Hall was sloshing through the river calling forth his son's name with every sloshy step. I called to him, "Mr. Hall! Hey, Mr. Hall!" For a moment he looked up at me, and the first thing that struck me was his forehead, which was as firmly wrinkled as a washboard. I told him about Philip's talking about being the King of the Mountain, but Mr. Hall didn't seem to pay any attention. I tried again, "We ought to be searching for Philip on that there mountain."

Next I tried my own pa, who didn't seem any more interested in what I was saying than Mr. Hall did. Now everybody was running down by the riverside frantically seeking somebody who wasn't no more there than the Monster of the Mountain.

Luther was always one who listened to good common sense. I found him and Ginny trying to look deep down into the river's bottom. When I told him how Philip had hung onto the bus's luggage rack to proclaim himself King of the Mountain, Luther looked at me only long enough to look confused. He had already returned to his search when I called out, "I'm going up that mountain to bring Philip down."

Past the picnic grounds there were acres of farmland that first had to be passed through. Over yonder a ways, a red tractor worked its way through the field. The base of the mountain didn't look all that far away until I started walking toward it, and then, after I'd walked for quite a spell and then a good spell longer, I finally reached that point where the land begins its climb.

Once I started up the tree-on-tree mountain, the day dropped into shadow and the now pine-scented air suddenly changed from pretty warm to pretty cool. And just as quickly my confidence got traded in for something else. Something less than confident. How was I going to find one medium-sized boy among a jillion acres and a trillion pines?

Remembering the movies and what the Indians do, I put my ear to the ground and listened. I heard the earth's heartbeat—or was it merely my own? I heard water rushing downstream and a nightingale's sad song, but I didn't hear nothing of no Philip Hall.

My knees, even more than my feet, grew tired. Never mind that. Had to go on. With every step I began to wish for a speedy train that could zip me up the mountain. And I even made a wish that I had never in my life laid eyes upon huaraches. My right heel was forming a blister, sure enough. A large damp leaf between the heel and the strap, though, helped out.

The coolness became cooler while the shadows became more shadowy. I called out *"Philip!"* and the sound of my own voice scattering the quietness scared me.

I sat down on the pine-needled ground to listen, rest, and decide whether to turn back or keep going. It was a hard decision to make. But figgering out what I did wrong was easier. Baby Benjamin could figger that one out as good as me. Imagine somebody dumb enough to go rushing off alone on some mountain looking for some boy who might not be there. King of the Mountain, my foot! He may be way downriver right now trying to teach minnows to swim through the narrow mouth of a Nehi bottle. Or snoozing away high up on the bus's luggage rack. And who would ever think to look for him there?

After a while the shady coolness gets to a person. Wish I had my sweater from home. Wish I was home. I tried rubbing away the turkey-pimples (Pa always says: Why give the glory to the goose?), but it began to feel as though the only thing that I was rubbing away was my own skin. Enough of that. And enough of this mountain! I'm going back down!

As I stood brushing the pine needles from my shorts, I heard a sound—it might have been a cry. I listened hard but I didn't hear it anymore. Just imagining? No! There it is! And it's coming from up the mountain. It was a Philip Hall moan! "Philip," I hollered up the mountain. "*Phil-ip Hall,* is that you?"

I began running up the mountain. The pine needles were a little slippery under the soles of my huaraches. "PHILIP!" Why didn't he answer me? This time I cupped my hands around my mouth just the way Luther does when he's calling his precious pigs. "Phil-ip, oh, Phil-ip! Can you hear me a-calling?"

This time I was lucky. A tear-soaked voice called back, "Beth! That Beth?"

"Sure enough is!" I yelled back just before coming to a granite boulder so wall-like that only God himself could have ever moved it. As I went around the immovable wall, I got my directions just a bit off. Nothing serious. Which way did I come from? And which way was I going? Here the mountain rose so gently that I couldn't be sure it was rising at all.

"Where are you, Philip?"

A whimper of a voice called back, "Here."

The pine trees grew closer and the light was dimmer.

"Where here?"

"Here here."

Philip sounded as though he were behind me. But how could that be if I'm facing up mountain? Well, what if I'm not? I'd have to listen carefully. In all four directions, I sang out. "Philip, keep talking."

"What do you want me to talk about?" he asked.

"Count backward from a hundred."

"One hundred . . . ninety-nine . . . ninety-eight . . ."

By the time Philip had reached ninety, I had found his direction. I'd walk a few steps and then stop and listen. "Seventy-nine . . . seventy-eight . . ." Reckon I must be getting closer 'cause his voice is getting louder. Trees, underbrush, and ever shadier shade, though, ain't helping none. "Fifty-two . . . fifty . . . forty-nine."

And there he was sitting up against a tree, big as life. When I spoke his name, he lit up happier than he'd ever lit up before. But that lasted only a moment. The next moment he was turning his eyes and finally his head from me.

"Ain't you pleased that I came up here looking for you?" Philip didn't answer, just kept his head turned away from me. I didn't know what to think unless he's thinking that I came up here to be King of his Mountain. Well, that's plumb ridiculous and I was just about to tell him so when I noticed his foot.

Swollen like I don't know what and shades darker than it had any right to be. "Oh, Philip, you hurt yourself."

He turned to face me. Even in this soft light his eyes looked red. "A branch tripped me. I fell against a rock . . . and it hurts too."

"It sure must hurt," I said, wishing I knew how we were going to get down this mountain. Philip's half crippled and I'm half lost. Boy!

"You ain't got nothing to eat on you, have you?" asked Philip, looking around for a plate of pie and a bag of sandwiches.

I dug into the pocket of my cut-off jeans to show that there wasn't nothing there, but instead found two fruit-flavored Lifesavers and an unwrapped (but unchewed) Chiclet. "You didn't eat no lunch," I said.

He took my offering. "Reckon I don't need you to tell me that."

"Can you walk on that leg?"

Philip shook his head no. "It even hurts when I'm not walking."

"Well, what if you put your weight on a crutch instead of on your bad foot?"

His eyes now darted around for the crutch same way they had a moment ago darted around for the pie and sandwiches.

"I didn't bring it," I explained. "I'm going to *be* it. So just flop your arm around my neck and lean on me." And we started out, with him raising his bad left foot slightly off the ground. "One good step, one bad step, one good step, one . . ."

"Why do you keep saying that?" he asked.

"Don't exactly know . . . excepting it sounds like we're making progress." What I didn't know was that Philip weighed so much. Once we reached the boulder I told him I had to sit and rest a spell.

"You're some fine crutch," he said, managing a little laugh while giving me a poke with what had to be his good foot.

"Reckon there are worse crutches," I said, not really wanting to spend any more energy on talk. " 'Cause I don't reckon you was doing much laughing before I came up here to fetch you."

Soon we were back, walking our strange three-legged

walk, but we hadn't been at it very long before my shoulder felt as though it was fixing to break off from under Philip's weight. "Rest," I called, letting him slowly bring himself down to sitting.

"We don't hardly get nowhere," he complained, "before you're ready to rest."

"Anyone ever tell you you weigh mite near a ton?" I answered, while thinking of other things I could have said. Things like, when was the last time you tried carrying some overgrown boy on your shoulders? Or this: It ain't me that's slowing me down. Reckon I could have said those things and more, but I didn't have neither the strength nor the heart for it. Besides, all I wanted to do . . . all I was able to do . . . was just to lie here with my body resting against God's good earth.

Walking again, I got to remembering how Tarzan swung from tree to tree across the entire African continent without once touching ground. I looked overhead. But Arkansas pines weren't growing no ropes. Not this season.

From time to time Philip would show the way by gesturing to the right or to the left, but otherwise he, like me, didn't have nothing to say.

When we finally reached the mountain's base, Philip and I celebrated by falling exhausted to the ground for still another rest. And this time our rest lasted longer and he didn't seem any more anxious to get moving again than me.

And when I finally got to my feet, I still felt tired as a toad, and the picnic area was a long way from being close.

This time was different in another way too. All those other times I rose from my rest saying to myself that I had to go on . . . had to be Philip's good strong crutch. But those were the other times. This time I can't help anybody. My own back feels as crippled as Philip's foot. Even without his weight hanging across my shoulders, I wouldn't make it back for help.

I pointed to the idle red tractor that had earlier been working this field. "Reckon you could drive that thing, Philip?"

"Sure," he said as though he'd never been surer of anything in his whole life.

I thought about the pain that came with each step. "How many steps over to it?" I asked.

"Not many."

"How many you reckon ain't many?"

This time he raised his head to make a more thoughtful appraisal. "Ohhh . . . not many."

"Let's go," I said, helping him to his feet. As he flopped his arm across my shoulder I shouted out, "Ohh! . . . two . . . three . . ." I expected his every breath to carry a complaint about my counting. "Eighteen . . . nineteen . . . twenty . . ." Maybe he understood that I had to keep my mind off the pain and on the progress. "Thirty-five . . . thirty-six . . . thirty-seven . . ." But Philip didn't say a word. "Forty-five . . . forty-six . . ." Then at the forty-seventh step we reached out and together touched tractor!

Philip pulled himself up into the seat and began working the levers on the right side of the steering wheel. One of the levers he pushed up, saying, "Advance the sparks," and the other lever he pushed down, saying, "Down the magneto." Then he looked down at me and yelled, "Go give her the crank!"

I went around in front and gave the old tractor a turn, but nothing happened. "Come on now, sweet thing," I coaxed, giving her crank another turn or two. "Don't you go acting up on us." Then, with the last bit of energy that God gave me, I gave her a good turn or two or three, and glory be, the motor started.

I crowded next to Philip on the driver's seat and watched as he pushed the shift stick down and drove off toward the picnic grounds. "Yea!"

As Philip drove into the grounds, the Reverend Ross looked about as surprised as if he was seeing one of them Bible miracles he's always preaching about. "First Lazarus!" cried out the minister. "And now Phil Hall! Glory bee!"

Farther on, Bonnie and Gordon were grass sitting, looking as though they had lost their dearest friend. "How-dy!" yelled Philip as he drove a wide circle around them. All four eyes pressed forward as though the center of gravity was Philip Hall.

"What's the matter with them?" Philip asked. "Haven't they never seen no tractor before?" He headed the old ma-

chine down toward the river. At water's edge, folks sat with their heads down between their hands while a few others dabbed at their eyes with soggy handkerchiefs.

Philip pointed out his mother, who stood staring at the river, hands pressed against her heart. "How-dy, Ma!" he called out. "What you got good to eat?"

Mrs. Hall stared at her son with unblinkable eyes before dropping to her knees. "Thank you, Lord! Oh, thank you, Lord!"

Philip moved the levers together and the motor died. As I climbed down, Mrs. Hall caught me in a bear-smothering hug. "You brought him back, Beth! You brought my boy back!" Then she pointed a finger at her youngest son, saying, "You had us so worried we mite near lost our minds. I ain't talking to you till my heart calms down!" She walked away faster than I had ever seen her walk.

While from the height of his tractor seat, Philip looked down at me like a little boy lost. "Can't figger whether she is loving me or hating me."

"Well . . ." I said, stalling till I got it straight in my own mind. "She hates the terrible scare you gave her, but we— I mean she—loves you, Philip Hall. I reckon maybe."

The calf-raising contest

September

We faced the green cloverleaf poster with the H on every leaf and with the strength of our fifteen voices recited:

> *I pledge my head to clearer thinking*
> > *my heart to greater loyalty*
> > *my hands to greater service and*
> > *my health to better living*
> *for my club, my community, and my country.*

Philip Hall struck the table with his gavel, which is pretty much the way the 4-H Club of Pocahontas, Arkansas, is always called to order. He asked everybody—one at a time—to tell how their project was coming along and if it was going to be ready for next Saturday's county fair.

Although my hand was the first raised, Philip was nodding toward Bonnie Blake, which was just as well, seeing as she had already begun talking. She told about the special problem of making a dress with a printed pattern, and then she explained with detail piled on top of boring detail how she overcame every single obstacle before concluding with: "But it's all finished now and I'm ready for the judging."

Waving my hand as hard as I could didn't help none 'cause our president had begun motioning toward Ginny, who got to her feet so slowly that you'd think she was the only one waiting to speak her piece. Then she did a powerful lot of explaining about all the trouble she went through getting a few garden vegetables into sealed jars before she finally said, "But my carrots, stewed tomatoes, and lima beans can't hardly wait for the canning contest."

I thought for sure I was going to be next, but Gordon was being asked to report on what he was doing to get himself prepared for the tractor maintenance contest. "Through the mail I got me this little booklet called *Maintaining Your John Deere Tractor* and I read it, top to bottom."

For a long time now Gordon's been working on Saturdays at the Randolph County Tractor Center and all us

4-H members think that if any one of us comes home with a blue ribbon (or even a red one) it is going to be him.

Next thing I knew, the Jones boys—Jordan and Joshua —were standing up explaining their pig's progress by weight and inches. Just when I got to thinking that that little pig is going to grow into a full-size hog before Jordan and Joshua finish up their explaining, the double Js did something truly amazing—they finished up their explaining.

Philip Hall smiled like folks do when they have been saving the best for last. He was fixing to call upon me. Ain't he a sweet thing? This time I didn't wave my hands. 'Cause when he tells the club about all the good work I'm doing with my calf Madeline, well, I'm going to act surprised and a little embarrassed.

But he began: "I named my female calf Leonard because Leonard doesn't act like no girl. Leonard's as brave as any bull and smart—Ooooooeeeeee!"

I couldn't hardly believe what I was hearing from that low-down polecat! I told him, "When Leonard gets grown he's going to be giving milk, more like a Leonora than a Leonard."

Everybody laughed except our president, who didn't find my remarks the least bit amusing. He didn't even wait for the laughing to end before going on with his talk. "Up to the time Leonard was ten days old he wouldn't put nothing in his mouth but mother's milk. So before feedings, I got to rubbing a little milk-soaked grain on his nose. Naturally enough, he'd lick it right off and that's how I tricked Leonard into liking grain."

When Philip paused long enough to let it sink in on everybody just what a fine calf-raiser he is, I waved my hands while bouncing up and down in my chair. But our president only began talking on about the importance of bone meal in Leonard's diet.

I wasn't listening. I was thinking back, remembering how he never ever let me say one word about my Madeline. And I know I tried explaining it to him that as long as our only cow, Maude, was calving, I might as well take care of her calf for my 4-H project. Even Pa remarked that it would be good learning for a future veterinarian.

Part of the problem with Philip is that he doesn't like the idea that our Old Maude with the sagging back could give birth to a calf good enough to compete with the very best from the Hall Dairy Farm. And another part of the problem has to do with boys and how they hate losing . . . especially how they hate losing to girls.

When Philip paused, I jumped to my feet. "Mr. 4-H President," I called out. "Reckon you is going to get around to calling upon me?"

"Speak your piece," said Philip, "if you have to."

"Well, Madeline is a Jersey cow and Jerseys, as any fool can tell you, don't come as big as Holstein or Guernsey cows. She didn't weigh but fifty pounds the day she was born and most Holsteins I know wouldn't bother coming into this world less'n they weighed least a hundred."

"Is you going to talk about all the cows that ever lived?" asked Philip.

"Reckon I can't tell you nothing while you keep butting in." I waited till I was right sure that Philip wasn't going to backsass me before going on. "You can't go around expecting a Jersey to weigh as much as a Holstein. It'd be the same thing as expecting a pea to weigh as much as a pear. Well," I said, making that a very long word, "according to the United States Department of Agriculture, it's real good if a three-month-old calf weighs one hundred and thirty-eight pounds, but do you know how much my Madeline weighs?"

"Nope!" answered Philip as though he didn't know and didn't care to know.

"My Madeline's weight is now"—I paused to let the suspense build—"one hundred and fifty pounds."

Ginny clapped and Bonnie said, "Twelve pounds to the good."

Philip waved everybody quiet. "Don't go counting your blue ribbons before you win any, Miss Beth!"

Did I have me a thing or two to tell him! "You've been acting plumb miserable ever since my Madeline is trying for the same prize that your Leonard is."

"You saying that Leonard and me is scared of Madeline and you?" Philip tried laughing. "Ha ha ha ha!" But it wasn't what you'd call a real laugh.

I stood tall in front of him and the rest of the 4-H members saying, "I thinks you is at least half-right," before moving on toward the door. Our president's face showed that he needed a mite more explaining so I gave it to him. "I don't think your Leonard is one bit scared, but I think you, Mr. Philip Hall, is downright terrified."

During supper, my mama complained that I must have left my appetite at the 4-H Club 'cause "You ain't eating enough to feed a poult." When I answered by saying that it was only Madeline on my mind, I caught her looking at me sideways. Like she does when she's stopped believing.

After sundown I carried the kerosene lamp quietly through the barn toward Madeline's stall. "Hello, sweet thing," I called, holding up a slab of cornbread. With a damp, sandpapery tongue, she pushed the treat off my hand into her waiting mouth.

I told Madeline, "Don't you be like Ma, thinking I'm upset just because that boy behaves the way he do!" I said, bringing my fist down upon her head. Madeline made what sounded like half of a moo before backing into the far corner of her pen.

What have I done! "Oh, sweet Madeline, I wouldn't hurt you for the world. It's only that low-down polecat who's got me steamed up with the mads."

The calf seemed to understand because she moved back toward me. For a while I stood stroking her head and thinking of another head I'd like to smack. The dumb bum! Where in the good book is it written that a girl's calf can't be in the same contest with a boy's calf? Well, Mister Philip Hall, for too long I've worried that you wouldn't like me if I became the number-one best student, ran faster in the relay race, or took the blue ribbon for calf-raising.

Well, I reckon I'm still worried, but with a difference. Now I'm worried that I might not win and that would give you entirely too much satisfaction.

By eight o'clock Saturday morning, all of us Lamberts, especially including Madeline the calf, got aboard Pa's pickup truck and headed for Mountain Village and the annual Randolph County Fair. In the back of the truck Luther and I stood on either side of Madeline and took turns building her confidence. I told her, "You're bound to win, sweet Madeline." And Luther contributed, "Madeline, you is a born blue-ribbon calf if ever I did see one."

Fifteen miles later Pa parked in front of a makeshift gate. Then with Luther shoving a reluctant Madeline from behind, I led her down the truck's plank.

Inside the early morning fair grounds everybody was busy rushing to set up their egg, vegetable, poultry, flower, or clothing exhibits. Folks with livestock were leading them toward the barn, so Madeline and I followed.

A big man who wore the sign, WM. PAULSEN, CATTLE JUDGE, pointed to a long shed behind a circle of temporary fencing. "Take your calf in there, girlie, and start preparing for the judging."

One thing I never did like was being called "girlie."

About the only folks who do that are big fat men. How would they like it if we girlies got to calling them "manlies"?

I gave the rough old rope harness a pull, and Madeline followed me into the barn past stalls filled with boys and their calves. At the first empty one, Madeline and I entered and then she looked at me with earth-colored eyes as if to ask, what's next?

"I'm going to make you beautiful for the judges," I explained as I rubbed brown shoe polish across her hooves. "You really are beautiful, sure enough." Those eyes looked as though they'd seen most all the problems under the heavens and after a mite more consideration, they'd be ready to offer up the solutions.

After I buffed her hooves with a piece of an old flannel shirt, I got out Madeline's hairbrush. Brushing is what really puts the shine on.

I heard the fat voice of the manlie in the distance saying, "Nice animal you got there, son." Walking with Mr. Paulsen was Philip Hall holding onto the polished leather bridle of a prettily spotted Holstein.

I said, "Leonard!"

Philip looked up.

"Philip," I said.

And Leonard looked up.

"Well, Philip," I said, trying for another start, "your Leonard looks real good. You sure did fatten him up." Considering the bad feeling between us, I silently congratulated myself on finding such a nice thing to say. But I've noticed that ever since my twelfth birthday last month I've been at times surprisingly grown-up.

Philip smiled wide enough to show the world how proud he was. "You know this here Leonard wouldn't eat a thing the first ten days of his life that wasn't mother's milk. Bet you wouldn't know what to do with an animal like that."

He's all the time forgetting that he told folks what he already told them. "Well . . . ," I said, pretending to be thinking. "Well . . . reckon I might try soaking some grain with milk and rubbing it across the animal's nose."

He looked at me as though I had taken something very important away from him. "How did you know?"

I laughed at him. " 'Cause you told that to everybody at the 4-H Club, you old forgetful head."

He punched the air. "Calf-raising is for boys and Leonard's going to beat the pants off Madeline."

"Says who?" I asked, which was a silly thing to ask since nothing could be plainer.

He threw out his chest. "Says me!"

I held tight onto Madeline's ragged old bridle. "Well, I don't hear me nobody talking. Don't hear me nothing except a big bag of wind."

Philip stuck out his tongue as he gave Leonard's bridle such a let's-get-out-of-here jerk that I was pleasantly surprised to find that poor calf's head somehow managed to stay attached to his body.

At ten o'clock all the exhibits from the dairy animals to

the flowers, foods, and crafts were ready and so Mr. Paulsen went on out to the front gate and told the crowd to "Come on in!" Around about noontime the entire fair grounds was packed with what looked like every living soul in Randolph County. And some of my favorite Randolph County souls, the Pretty Pennies, came by our stall to wish us luck and to remind us how important it is to "beat Phil and Leonard."

I noticed that the Tiger Hunters went by Leonard's stall and it wouldn't be too hard for a smart girl like me to guess what those Tiger Hunters were advising.

"Well, they're not going to beat us," I said as I held Madeline's tail lengthwise to brush it with the now half-bald brush. " 'Cause I don't aim to let them."

Mr. Paulsen walked through the long barn calling, "The judging is about to commence."

I gave Madeline one last brush across her backside before unwrapping the secret weapon. A package of peppermint Lifesavers. A sweet breath can't hurt none. Right away she took it and right away she spit it out, but not before it freshened up her mouth a mite.

The line began moving. I counted seven boys and me. And wouldn't you know who was out there leading the parade? Out there wearing his new leather harness and holding his head high as any clothesline. Funny, but I ain't liking Leonard any better than I'm liking Philip Hall.

All of us exhibitors walked backward so we could face our animals, seeing to it that they kept their heads high and mighty, leastways while the judge is a-looking. Once around the ring as bits and pieces of applause broke out from the spectators. Judge Paulsen motions for us all to go around again while he stays center-ring and watches. Once more he motions for us all to round-the-rosie, and this time the clapping is louder and longer. I thought about how a piece of that clapping had to belong to me, and I felt proud.

I looked away from Madeline to see if Ma, Pa, Luther, and Anne could be quickly spotted in the crowd. Wanted to see if they—like me—were wearing pride's faces.

Only one I saw was my sister with Jason Savage on her right and Herbie Ferrell on her left. I yelled out, *"How-dy."*

And then I heard Luther's voice shouting over all the other ringside voices, *"Watch her!"* Right away I saw the problem. Madeline had dropped her head for a few juicy between-meals blades of grass.

I jerked her up by the rope halter. "Miserable Madeline! Ain't no manners worse than eating while a judge is a-judging." Luck may still be riding with us, though, 'cause Judge Paulsen, back against us, is checking on the cleanliness of some animal's hooves. Under my breath I thanked the Lord for giving me this new chance.

I looked into the eyes of my beautiful calf and made this sucking-in sound with my mouth. The sound that Madeline understands as friendly. "You ain't one bit miserable," I told her. "And I is sorry that I blamed you, sweet girl, for what was only animal nature."

The judge slapped one calf across the rump and pointed with his thumb toward the open stalls. The calf's boy looked hurt beyond belief, as he led his animal from the ring. Then the judge passed by Leonard to give the following calf the old rump slap and the hitchhiker's thumb. The very next one, poor thing, came in for the same treatment.

When Madeline came before the judge's eyes, I breathed in and kept my mind and eyes on her, praying that the judge was going to let us pass on by. The judge's head made a very definite nod which I took to mean that Madeline was still in the contest.

After more walks around the ring a Guernsey and one Jersey, but not my Jersey, were sent from the ring. Who was left? A cherry-red-and-white Ayrshire, Leonard, and Madeline.

Mr. Paulsen was studying the Ayrshire, pressing his hands against the ribs, feeling its udder and then its chest. Suddenly he shook his head no and pointed the direction toward the barn. Farewell fancy Ayrshire!

As Philip led his animal around the opposite turn, he gave me one of his squinty looks that I read good as print. It said: Now there is only you and me, but soon it's going to be only me.

I didn't squint him back any special look because just now I had better things to do. I made the whistle-through-my-teeth sound and Madeline's head rose, ever so slightly, as though searching for the wind. I did it again. That's it.

Keep your head up there, girl. Makes you look like the sweet-breath winner that you is.

For the second time Leonard and then Madeline was carefully examined. Through the corner of my eye I saw Judge Paulsen's hand go to his chin as though thought was deep upon him. For a while he stared at Leonard and then he stared at Madeline, and all the while I kept the wind whistling so softly that it only existed for Madeline.

The judge motioned Philip and me to bring our calves to the center ring. "Ladies and gentlemen . . . ladies and gentlemen. We have a winner." I struck my chest so as my heart wouldn't stop beating. "The blue ribbon for dairy-calf-fitting goes to the exhibitor who has best taken care of *and* shown to best advantage their calf. It is now my very great honor to present the blue ribbon and five dollars to Miss Elizabeth Lorraine Lambert for her three-month-old calf, Madeline."

Applause and it was all mine. Then the voices of my friends began chanting, "GO, PRET-TY PEN-NY . . . GO, PRET-TY PEN-NY, GO!" And over there Ma and Pa clapping hard enough to raise the thunder. Even Baby Benjamin waved a hand in my direction and I knew that if he could, he'd be calling my name.

Judge Paulsen raised his arms above his head for quiet and that's exactly what he got. He announced Philip as second-place winner for a red ribbon and three dollars, but there wasn't all that much clapping, and even the Tiger

Hunters who gave out with a "Phil and Leonard" chant didn't seem to throw their whole hearts into it. Philip was looking down, not from modesty, but from shame. Was he thinking that he had let down the whole world—or just the Tiger Hunters at the very least?

Folks flooded into the show ring. Ma was the first one to reach me, not really hugging me but holding me at a distance as though to get a better look at what a blue-ribbon exhibitor really looks like. "Never knowed where you got all your smartness from, Little Beth, but I couldn't hardly be no prouder than I am right now."

"Awww, Mama," I said, dropping my head to her shoulder so that she couldn't see the tear or two that had begun irritating my eyes. I had made her happy. I had done just what I had set out to do. So why was I fretting?

She pulled me away from her and took another long look before saying, "Phil ain't gonna be mad forever."

"You don't think so?" I asked, already beginning to believe.

"I don't go strutting around saying things I don't believe," she said. "Besides, it being you, you couldn't hardly do nothing but what you did do—your best."

"Howdy, Miss Beth!" called Pa, grabbing me by the waist and giving me a free swing about.

When Fancy Annie came up holding Baby Benjamin, I took him in my arms and he showed his thanks by drooling a kiss down my cheek, which is a lot pleasanter than one of his sour-milk burps down my shoulder.

The next thing I noticed was my friends dropping to one knee as they formed a circle around me, my family, and Madeline. "Together now," called out Bonnie. "Go, Pret-ty Pen-ny . . . Go, Pret-ty Pen-ny . . . Go, Pret-ty Pen-ny. GO! GO! GO!" Then they all jumped to their feet shouting, "Hooray Beth! Hoo-ray Lambert! Hoo-ray Beth Lambert! HOO-RAY!!!"

Later all us Pretty Pennies walked about the fair grounds while encouraging Ginny to believe that her canned carrots looked every bit as good as anybody else's and that with a bit of luck she might win a blue ribbon too.

When folks saw me, they smiled, nodded, and offered up their congratulations. It was nice being all that special; still . . . there was one person whose face I kept searching for, whose smile I kept hoping for. Would it hurt him to be nice? For once in his life? Well, just don't go thinking I care!

The very next contest was the sewing, and all us girls had every finger and limb crossed for Bonnie's gabardine dress with the Peter Pan collar. But a girl from Mountain Village whose dress wasn't a bit prettier than Bonnie's won the blue ribbon and if that wasn't bad enough, another girl from the very same town came in second for a red ribbon. After that came the honorable mentions, but poor Bonnie went unhonored and unmentioned.

But a few minutes later, when we all ordered hot dogs

and Nehi's from the lunch wagon, Bonnie ate good enough to make me think that if she was taking defeat to heart, she stopped short at taking it to stomach.

At one o'clock the canning contest began and when the woman judge began examining the glass jars, Ginny became as nervous as a cow fixing to calve. I grabbed ahold of my friend's arms and gave them a shaking. "Quiet yourself down. Ain't no end of no world a-coming."

But when Ginny's glass jar of canned carrots was passed over without ribbons or mentions, she became strangely relaxed. "I tried to push in too many carrots. Next year they ain't going to be squeezed."

The two o'clock event was the tractor maintenance contest, and the crowd moved over to the area where there were six tractors each with the very same secret ailment and six boys with identical sets of tools. At the whistle they all began searching for the fault. Six minutes later Gordon Jennings was the first to replace a missing spark plug and win the contest while the entire Pocahontas 4-H Club chanted his praises.

When I saw Philip Hall, I tried to ease across the crowd to where he was, but when I got to where he was, he wasn't. Don't go thinking I care!

At the start of evening the lights strung about the grounds flashed on. A huge flatbed of a truck decorated to look like a stage wore a long banner sign: WELCOME SKINNY BAKER, KING OF THE SQUARE-DANCE CALLERS.

I reminded the girls what nobody on the whole fair

grounds needed to be reminded of. "Square dancing oughta be starting up soon." As we wandered off to the side to "pretty ourselves up," Bonnie told us a secret. Gordon was going to be her partner. Then Ginny, Susan, and Esther admitted that they had been keeping the same secret, only with different partners.

Fact is, there was only one Pretty Penny who didn't have a secret to tell 'cause not even a blue-ribbon winner can swing a partner she hasn't got.

When Skinny Baker struck up his do-si-do band, the girls jumped to their feet as though scared silly that they might miss a single square-dancing step. As they ran off toward the lights and the music, I sat in the darkness and wondered, what now?

For a while I watched the stars and waited for them to arrange themselves into a pattern spelling out in capital starlit letters exactly what I should or shouldn't do. I thanked God in advance for all the trouble he was about to go through on my account, and I told him that there wasn't any real rush. "You can take your time, Lord. Five, even ten minutes would be fine with me."

I lay back across the grass and closed my eyes (peeking is cheating) and waited for the miracle of the stars to happen. It wouldn't even be a problem knowing when the ten minutes are up because I remember Ma sometimes times her eggs by songs played over the radio. Each song is three minutes' worth.

So when Skinny Baker finished up his third song and got

a ways into the fourth, I called out, "Here I come, God, ready or not!" I opened my eyes and searched the sky for the starry message that would be waiting there. East, west, north, south. It wasn't there. Nowhere.

I spoke in the direction of the star that looked the biggest and bossiest. "Reckon I don't rightly know, Lord, where you got this reputation for answering prayers."

I stood up, brushing the grass off my clothes as I spoke again. "Well, iffen you're not going to spell out what I ought to do, then I'm going to have to use my God-given brains to do what I think I oughta."

I came out of the darkness toward the lights and the music and looked among the faces for his face. The jerk. I hope I never see him again.

Over there dancing up a storm was my ma and pa. I didn't know they could still do that. And would you look at Fancy Annie and Jason Savage? Don't take no telling to tell they is sweet on each other. All the Pretty Pennies were being swung about by some Tiger Hunter. It seemed as though the whole world was dancing, with the exception of one Pretty Penny and one Tiger Hunter who was nowhere to be seen.

Well, if he wasn't out dancing down the grass, then maybe he was one of the watchers who lined the field. I circled, looking everybody over from the backside. I saw a lot of backsides, only not his.

With everybody paired as though waiting to enter the ark, being separate was noticeable. "Well, Madeline," I said, heading back toward the barn, "now that you is the champ, reckon you have time to listen to my troubles?"

Almost as soon as my foot struck the barn floor, I saw her fawn-colored head rise above her slatted stall. "You're looking good enough," I told her, "to pose for one of those advertisements about them 'contented cows.' "

I put my arms around her neck and spoke directly into her spoon-shaped ear, "I like winning the blue ribbon, sure do, but I don't like losing my best friend." Madeline made a sound which I took to be friendly sympathy, so I went on. "Why should he fault me 'cause I do things better than other folks? I've always been that way—you can ask my ma."

As soon as I said that, the thought struck me that it ain't likely that Madeline will ever ask that or any other question. But I just went on talking hurriedly so she wouldn't take no notice of my mistake. "And so, Madeline," I told her, "I know I wouldn't be carrying on so if he had won the blue ribbon and I had only won the red one. I wouldn't be one bit mad—and that's the truth!"

Suddenly there was a lot of hoofing around a couple of stalls down. I looked up in time to see the face of Philip Hall rise above Leonard's slatted gate. Reckon I was too surprised to do anything, excepting stare. He wasn't smiling, speaking, or looking in any way pleasant, but then he wasn't exactly looking altogether unpleasant either. Then he said something. It was "Hi."

I answered with a "Hi" of my own. And neither of us

seemed to be able to go on from there. Philip was looking down inspecting the floor while I was looking up counting the beams. It felt as though talking was something that neither of us had yet learned to do.

Suddenly I couldn't take another moment like the last one. "Sorry!" I heard myself saying. "I should've let you win."

Philip fastened his hands to his hips. "And you think that's what I want!" He was doing more telling than asking. "Think I'm some baby other folks have to *let* win?"

"No, Philip. I only thought—"

"Truth is," he continued, "all you been doing lately is winning, and that ain't hard to live with. Hard thing is losing."

"Reckon so," I said.

"No, you done forgotten about losing," he said, " 'cause if you'd remembered you'd know full well that it takes getting used to."

"And are you getting used to it?" I asked. "I mean, a little?"

Philip nodded his head. "I ain't no baby."

"Reckon I know that," I told him, " 'cause I can see you growing." When I saw on his face the makings of a smile, I said, "Come on, we still have time to enter the square-dancing contest."

He stopped short. "I'm not about to enter no more contests with you, leastways not today."

"You don't understand, Philip. This contest is for partners. Win together or lose together."

"Sometimes I reckon I likes you, Beth Lambert," he said
as we touched hands and together ran toward the lights,
the music, and the microphone-amplified voice of Skinny
Baker.

Bette Greene grew up in a small Arkansas town and in Memphis, Tennessee. Her first novel, *Summer of My German Soldier*, won unanimous critical acclaim. She is also the author of *Get On Out of Here, Philip Hall*, the sequel to *Philip Hall Likes Me. I Reckon Maybe*. Bette Greene lives in Brookline, Massachusetts.

STINKER
FROM
SPACE

PAMELA F. SERVICE

CHARLES SCRIBNER'S SONS
NEW YORK

This novel is a work of fiction. Names, characters, places, and incidents are either the product of the author's imagination or are used fictitiously. Any resemblance to actual persons, living or dead, is entirely coincidental.

Copyright © 1988 by Pamela F. Service

Charles Scribner's Sons Books for Young Readers
Macmillan Publishing Company
866 Third Avenue, New York, NY 10022
Collier Macmillan Canada, Inc.

Printed in the United States of America
10 9 8 7 6 5

Library of Congress Cataloging-in-Publication Data
Service, Pamela F.
Stinker from space / Pamela F. Service.
p. cm.
Summary: An agent of the Sylon Confederacy, fleeing from enemy ships, crash lands on Earth, transfers his mind to the body of a skunk, and enlists the aid of two children in getting back to his home planet.
ISBN 0–684–18910–0
[1. Extraterrestrial beings—Fiction.   2. Skunks—Fiction.
3. Science fiction.]   I. Title.
PZ7.S4885St   1988   87–25266
[Fic]—dc19   CIP
                                AC

· FOR DOUG ·

CONTENTS

STINKER
FROM
SPACE

1

Fugitive

Again the deadly blue light engulfed him. Flinching from the brilliance, Tsynq Yr struggled with the controls. Abruptly his scout ship veered away, and the cool glow faded.

He knew he was a crack space pilot, one of the best in the Sylon Confederacy, but that Zarnk cruiser was closing on him fast. He was hopelessly outgunned and outpowered in this cheap scout ship he'd had to steal to escape the orbital fort. What he wouldn't give now for his own trim little Sylon fighter.

Blue radiance flared again, and Tsynq Yr abruptly changed the ship's course. He could not let them get him now. Three years of miserable skulking and spying, and finally he'd pieced it all together. He'd found out the Zarnk plan for attacking the Delta Arm of the Confederacy. He must get that information back to Sylon High Command, and he wasn't about to let a blundering Zarnk cruiser stop him.

The cramped cabin burst into blue glare. On Tsynq Yr's right, the control panel fizzed and crackled.

He surveyed the damage. Now that's done it! The stabilizers were out. There was only one choice left, he realized, and he didn't like it. The maneuver was difficult and dangerous at the best of times. In this piece of flying space scrap. . . .

Before the Zarnk could fire again, Tsynq Yr slid the drive control to the top of the scale, well beyond the safety limit. The little ship shuddered and shot off through space. With the rising speed, the blackness around him began to waver and vibrate as he neared the fringes of hyperspace. This ship was not equipped to make the jump into that dimension, but with skillful piloting and split-second timing, it skipped along the dimensional boundaries like a stone skips over water.

Tensely Tsynq Yr played the controls. If he didn't obliterate himself, this little trick should throw off pursuit for a time, enough time perhaps for him to repair the ship or find some Sylon reinforcements.

As space pulsed and shivered around the speeding ship, an alarming hum rose from the controls. That last Zarnk hit must have done more damage than he'd thought. Suddenly the hum turned into a scream and the ship abruptly lost speed, spinning off through black, star-spotted space.

When, with much cursing, he'd brought the spinning

under control, Tsynq Yr looked out at those stars. Where was he? Skipping along the edges of hyperspace played havoc with physical location, and he had no idea where he'd been dropped off. Of course, his pursuers wouldn't either, but that would be no help if he'd been plunked somewhere in the Zarnk Dominion.

But no, the stars showed he was in neither Zarnk nor Sylon territory. Terrific! Exploring uncharted regions was all very well, but not when he had top secret information to pass on.

A quick glance at the smoking control panel showed that here he was and here he was likely to remain, at least until he could work some repairs. He trained his scanners on the nearest star system. Planets, yes, mostly useless. One marginal, one fully habitable. He homed in on the latter.

If the Zarnk ever managed to trace his wild route here, this planet would be an all too obvious refuge, but he had no choice. His little ship was making new alarming sounds.

He sped toward the target, a globe swirling with greens and blues and whites. Pleasant-looking, all right, but too much water. With half the ship's systems out, this landing was going to be rough enough. Tsynq Yr hoped it would at least be on land.

Plummeting down toward the planet's night side, he knifed into the atmosphere. Too steep. He tried to pull up but failed. Worse, he seemed to be heading into a local storm system.

Dark clouds closed in. Everywhere the atmosphere

discharged in long forked bolts. Suddenly the ground, splotched with vegetation, was hurtling toward him. Too fast. Much too fast.

When Tsynq Yr awoke, he realized two things. First, his ship was nearly destroyed. Second, he was dying.

This body had served him well. At first, he'd taken it on merely as a convenience to his spy mission. Like most active Sylons, he'd lost track of how many bodies he'd used since the one he'd had at birth. But this body had worked well, was attractive in its own way—and he'd grown attached to it.

And he would die in it, too, if he didn't find a suitable host—soon. His mind cast about, seeking life forms. Vegetation was plentiful, but all seemed rooted and subintelligent. He sensed other creatures that did move, but he probed and found they weren't much more intelligent than the plants. Tiny flying creatures seemed interested only in finding out if his own dying body was good to eat.

Desperate now, he probed elsewhere. Here was something larger. It wriggled through the soil, but its brain was negligible. He doubted his intelligence could even fit into it. And besides, it had no appendages. He could never repair a ship in that body.

Suddenly the thing he probed at was snatched up and eaten by another creature. This new one would have to do. He hadn't the strength to look further. Yes, there was a brain, not a big one, but he'd worked with worse. And there were even hands of sorts.

With his last shred of strength, Tsynq Yr shot his being into the alien creature. The native's intelligence registered brief surprise before it was pushed to the back of the mind and the Sylon took over.

Beady black eyes blinked as he gazed at the alien world around him. Vegetation everywhere, tall and short, orange, brown, and green. Moisture blew from a clouded night sky. His eyes, it seemed, were designed for seeing in the near dark.

Curiously Tsynq Yr examined his new body. There was a head and a tail, and four short legs supporting a body that was low to the ground. Mammalian, apparently; the whole body was covered with hair.

That hair was clearly the most impressive feature. It was long, soft, and marked in a striking pattern. The background was glossy black. White capped the head, and two bold white stripes swept down the back and out onto the bushy plume of a tail. Quite handsome, really.

2

Meeting in the Woods

Dark Destroyer dropped in beside the Princess of Light. One by one the other action figures followed before Karen slammed down the lid.

Swinging the old battered lunchbox in one hand, she clattered down the stairs and into the kitchen. Her mother looked up, her face taut with the unfamiliar strain of sewing curtains.

"Going out to play?"

"Yes," Karen replied as she scooped several peanut butter cookies into her pocket.

Mrs. Blake's frustration over the curtains ricocheted against her daughter. "Karen, honestly! Why don't you ever play *with* anyone?"

"Oh, Mother! There's no one here I want to play with."

"We've been here two whole months n
Surely you've made some friends by now."

Karen swayed by the doorway, hand itching to
the knob. "Oh sure, some of the girls at school are oka
but they aren't like. . . . They don't play my sort of
games." She'd barely avoided saying "like Rachel." Her
mother had threatened to scream if she whined any
more about leaving her best friend behind in their old
hometown.

Karen sidled toward the door. "These girls just want
to dress up, put on makeup, and play with dolls."

"And those things in the lunchbox aren't dolls, I suppose?"

Karen sputtered indignantly. "These are action figures! They aren't silly dolls that wet and poop on de-
mand. They're characters in great interstellar dramas,
adventurers bounded only by imagination!"

She placed her hand on the doorknob and threw out
a line that was sure to divert her mother's train of
thought. "Besides, all the other girls live in town."

"Yes, your father *would* choose a picturesque 'handy-
man's delight' way out in the sticks." Mrs. Blake sighed
and gave the curtain an angry stab with her needle.
"But still, it's not completely isolated out here. Why don't
you play with that kid who lives up the road?"

"But he's a boy!"

"Well, I can't help that. Besides, if you're so nuts about
space, you two should be made for each other. I understand he's wacky over space, too."

ıme at all. When Jonathan Wal-
ne sees is numbers and facts—
ance!"

her mother seemed to ignore
lking with his mother the other
ıan's room is full of space posters
ıws the names of every astronaut,
ıce the year dot."

"There weren't any astronauts in the year dot."

"Talk about being too factual! Oh, go on out and play."

Quickly Karen slipped out the door. Last night's storm had polished the sky to a bright blue. Against it, the autumn colors of the woods ahead rose like a jeweled crown.

Freed from parental plans, she skipped toward those trees, heading for the hidden clearing she had already made her special place. But as she hopped over the rain puddles, she found herself still thinking about Jonathan Waldron.

He might be interested in space, but he was a real nerd nonetheless. All numbers and no soul. It was bad enough having to ride the bus with him. But be friends with him? In school Jonathan was a whiz in math and science, but hopeless in English. His poems stank. Of course, she thought with a giggle, boys stink generally. Still, she wouldn't mind seeing his room and all those models and posters.

Reaching the clearing, Karen dropped all unpleasant

thoughts. It was breathtakingly beautiful here. In the brilliant sunlight, the flaming red maple leaves glowed like stained glass. Settling down among the maple's gnarled roots, she leaned back and looked up at the gleaming leaves. She was a medieval princess taking refuge in an ancient cathedral. The stark white branches of the sycamore across the clearing were the soaring marble pillars. Or maybe she was a princess on another planet, taking refuge in the heart of the giant Sacred Jewel to escape the soldiers of the Dark Empire.

Opening the lunchbox, she spilled the action figures over the grass. Birds chirped busily in the leafy recesses of the woods. From a distance, the crisp air carried the tang of burning leaves. It mingled with the rich moldy odor of damp earth and fleeting whiffs of woodsy animals.

Although Tsynq Yr's first hours on this planet had been trying ones, he was fairly pleased with his new body. The creature's native intelligence was not high, but the brain was adaptable, and Sylon intelligence was very compact. And besides looking elegant, the little beast had some very interesting senses. Hearing and eyesight were keen, and there was another sense, the olfactory one, that he'd seldom had before. Life was suddenly full of interesting odors, not the least of which was his own.

The state of his ship, however, was far less satisfactory. It had smashed into the boggy earth, and the outside structure had all but disintegrated. Already the remains were sinking from sight. Somehow, he'd have to construct or borrow another vehicle.

That meant finding out something about the level of native civilization. During his fateful descent, the little ship's scanners had shown signs of civilization on this planet, but he had no idea how advanced it was.

He had set out to discover this about the time dawn came to this world, with its medium-size sun appearing in the east. His host's body was suddenly telling him it was time to sleep. He put aside that message easily enough, but messages from the empty stomach were harder to ignore.

His rations were gone with the ship, so he let his body's instincts take him to food. Soon he was industriously turning over dead logs and snapping up the bugs and fat white grubs underneath. He didn't dare let his own instincts rise to the surface, for fear he'd be instantly sick. Even so, the rotten raw bird's egg he ate was almost too much.

It was the smell of food enticing to both his selves that brought him to the clearing. Under a red-leafed tree, a bipedal creature was sitting, eating a round flat piece of food.

His mind as well as his sense of smell reached out, and instantly he realized that here was a species of considerable intelligence. Perhaps one of this planet's civilized beings. Artificial garments, large brain capacity. He probed into the thoughts.

There was a running account of soldiers of a vast interstellar empire pursuing the female monarch of a rival power. So these beings had achieved space travel. He was in luck!

He decided to make himself known—mentally. His new body clearly didn't have much speech ability. How should he start—ask what sort of space drive they used? Maybe he should inquire if they had any knowledge of the Sylon Confederacy or the Zarnk Dominion. Or maybe, part of him urged, he should just ask what the creature was eating.

"I am dreadfully hungry," he thought. "Would you share some of that?"

The girl looked startled, then muttered, "Karen, you dope, don't have Dark Destroyer ask for a peanut butter cookie."

"He wasn't asking, I was," came the thought as Tsynq Yr stepped into the clearing.

Karen's look of surprise changed to alarm. Slowly she stood up and began backing away.

The Sylon stopped advancing and studied her. She was clearly frightened—of him. Puzzled, he probed her mind. It had something to do with the olfactory sense. A word jumped to the front of her thoughts, a word with very negative associations. Skunk.

3

An Alliance

Karen backed up slowly. She didn't like abandoning her loyal band of action figures but was afraid any sudden move would startle the skunk into stinking at her.

"I won't stink at you!" came an indignant thought.

"You will, too. You're a skunk!" Karen shook her head violently. "Hold it, kid," she said to herself. "Better go play dress up with the other girls if you're going to start making up dialogue for skunks."

"You didn't make it up. I said that. But don't worry about your model creatures. My main interest at the moment is with the object you're eating."

Bewildered, Karen looked at the half-eaten peanut butter cookie in her hand. Hesitantly she threw it into the clearing. "Here," she said aloud. "But if you think I'm going to talk, or think, at animals that can't talk, you're crazy."

Tsynq Yr waddled toward the cookie and after an ecstatic sniff began munching, his thoughts unhindered by the crumbs in his mouth. "Delicious. But you are being most unreasonable. I am obviously not an animal that can't talk, since you are talking with me."

"You *are* an animal that can't talk!" she thought back. "You are a skunk, and skunks can't talk."

"Obviously, then, I am not a skunk. This is really very good. Have you got any more?"

Automatically her hand went to her pocket and she threw another cookie onto the grass. "So what are you then? You certainly look like a skunk. And smell like one, too, I bet." Suddenly she clenched her fists. "No! I will not talk, or *think,* at a skunk!" Deliberately she turned around and started walking away.

"Oh well, I suppose you aren't intelligent enough for curiosity."

"Don't you think insults at me!"

"You were thinking some pretty insulting things about my odor."

"That's because you're a. . . . Oh, this is impossible! All right, all right, what are you if you are *not* a skunk? And don't think I believe in you just because I'm thinking at you." She took a few steps back. The black and white creature in front of her was licking crumbs off the grass.

"First let me ask you if the terms Zarnk or Sylon are familiar to you."

"No, they're not." Mentally the answer felt honest to him. "But," she continued, "I asked you a question first."

"All right, then, I'll tell you. I'm in the Space Corps

of the Sylon Confederacy. A Zarnk cruiser was after me, and I had to oscillate along the hyperspace boundary to escape. My flimsy little scout ship was damaged, however, and I spun out into this sector. Then when I tried to land here for repairs the ship was completely wrecked. Now I need help getting off your planet."

"Oh," Karen said, sitting down again at the base of the tree. Her mind registered fear, fading into doubt, fading into interest and finally excitement. But there was no extreme surprise, confirming for Tsynq Yr that these people were familiar with space travel and extra-planetary life.

"So," Karen said aloud, leaning back against the tree trunk, "let me get this straight. You're a skunk from outer space, some bad guys are after you, and you need to get back to some place out there." She waved a hand vaguely at the leaf framed sky.

"Right. Except I am not really a skunk. I borrowed this body from a passerby. My earlier body was fatally injured in the crash."

"Wow," she said shaking her head. "Do you change bodies all the time?"

"No, not all the time. It takes too much energy. I only do it in dire need."

"Oh." She was silent a moment, then reached into her pocket. "Would you like another?"

"Yes indeed. What are they?" He ambled forward, his white striped nose twitching eagerly.

"They're cookies, made with peanut butter."

"Peanut butter?" His whiskers tickled her outstretched hand as, squatting on his hind legs, he retrieved another cookie. "I imagine I'd like this in any body. Maybe I should take some home with me."

Karen sat back and looked at the fat furry creature. Skunks were really kind of cute if you didn't worry about the stink. "So, how do you plan to get back if your ship's wrecked?"

"I was hoping you could help me with that."

"Me? I don't know anything about spaceships. I'm just a kid."

"An immature member of the species? Ah. Well, perhaps you could direct me to the nearest spaceport."

"Spaceport? We haven't any."

"No? But I thought. . . . Well, maybe what I should do first is learn a little about your civilization. You are certain, now, that you know nothing of the Zarnk Dominion?"

"Zarnk Dominion? No, never heard of it. Is it anything like the Dark Empire?"

He scanned her mind for the reference. "Yes, somewhat similar."

"Ah, real nasties. Well then, I guess I'll have to help you escape." She frowned thoughtfully for a minute. "If you want to learn more about Earth, maybe you could come home with me and read the encyclopedia. That has stuff about everything I've ever had to do a school paper on."

"Yes, perhaps that would be the wisest course. Do

you perhaps . . . uh, have any more peanut butter cookies at this home of yours?"

"Sure. Peanut butter cookies, and I think there are still some peanut butter–dip granola bars. And there's a jar of peanut butter, and some straight peanuts too if there are any left from my parents' party last week."

Mentally he sighed with contentment. "This body of mine seems to be constantly hungry."

Karen stood up and walked across the leaf-strewn clearing. Eagerly the skunk followed. In a few minutes they had emerged from the trees and started along a faint footpath in the weedy meadow. In the brilliant autumn sunlight, the skunk's black and white stood out boldly against the yellowed grass.

Karen turned and looked at her bizarre new companion. "Have you a name?" Deliberately she thought the question. This form of communication would take getting used to.

"Yes, I am called Tsynq Yr."

"Stinker?" She whooped with laughter. "Your name is Stinker?"

"No, no. Not pronounced like that. Tsynq Yr."

But she was laughing too hard to detect any difference. "Oh, that's perfect. Perfect!"

The Sylon thought he should probably be insulted, but if it amused this alien so much to mangle his name, he supposed it was acceptable. Particularly if she provided more of that peanut butter.

4

"Can We Keep Him?"

As Karen approached the old white farmhouse, it occurred to her that Stinker might not be a totally welcome guest. She decided to go around to the front door and make a direct dash for the hall stairs, hoping her mother was still struggling with curtains in the kitchen.

Leading the waddling skunk, she walked stealthily around the house to the front porch and quietly opened the door. Her mother was standing in the hall, a stricken look on her face.

"Karen," she whispered hoarsely, "I saw it from the window but was afraid to shout. Do you know there's a . . . a skunk following you?"

"Oh. Yes. His name is Stinker. He's . . . uh, someone's pet, I think. He's very tame."

"How do you know? Oh dear, he's coming in! Get him out of here before he sprays!"

"Really, he's very friendly, so he must be a pet. And I'm sure he's deodorized." She shot a thought at Stinker: "If you make a stink now, I'll skin you."

"Oh, but a skunk, Karen! Maybe he's rabid. That could be why he's not acting like a wild skunk." Her voice had a panicky edge.

"No, no, he must be somebody's pet. Look, he does tricks." She reached down and grabbed their dog's battered tennis ball from the floor, then bounced it along the hall. "Fetch!" she said pointedly.

Stinker got the picture.

Feeling like an idiot, he ambled after the ball, chasing it as it ricocheted off the umbrella stand. Eventually he threw himself on top of the thing. Then, managing to get his jaws around it, he carried it awkwardly back to Karen and laid it at her feet.

"There, you see?" she said pleadingly.

"Well. . . ."

Just then, Stinker heard toenails click on the floorboards behind him. He spun around and was gripped by an almost uncontrollable urge to lift his tail at the golden-haired creature behind him. But he caught a mental wave of horror from Karen and concentrated instead on trying to communicate with the thing.

"I'm a friend," he told it. "I belong here. I like you."

The spaniel whined and wagged his stump of a tail. Slowly it walked up and began smelling the skunk.

"We can have nice times together," Stinker continued at the dog. "We can play together, chase the ball, find loathsome things to eat."

The dog sat down in front of the newcomer and grinned amiably.

Karen's mother watched with amazement. "Well, will you look at that? I've never seen Sancho act like that with a strange animal. He's usually all stiff legs and growls."

"See? Stinker must be a pet. Perfectly safe and odorless. Can we keep him?"

"Well. . . . I suppose we'll have to keep him until we can find the owner." She stood for a moment looking thoughtfully at the skunk. "You know, he is kind of cute at that."

Stinker cringed at the word but decided he had better play up to it. This person was obviously an authority figure. Sitting on his broad hind end, he wrapped his tail around him and tucked his two forepaws under his chin.

"Don't overdo it," Karen thought at him.

Her mother's expression was quavering between a smile and a worried frown. "Oh dear, I don't know what to do. I guess your father could drop an ad by the newspaper office tomorrow on his way to work. But maybe we should just take the skunk to the animal shelter."

"Oh, no!"

"Well. . . . maybe not yet. But that's just until someone's had a chance to answer the ad. And, Karen, you have to take him on walks frequently. I hope he's housebroken."

"Oh, I'm sure he is," Karen said, adding the thought that he'd darn well better be.

"And it'll be your job to feed him. I wonder what skunks eat."

"Peanut butter," Karen answered without thinking.

"How do you know?"

"Oh, I read it someplace."

"Well, whatever. But taking care of him will be your responsibility entirely until we can see if someone answers the ad. Understand?"

"Yes, Mother. No problem. Let's go upstairs, Stinker."

As they trotted up the carpeted stairs, Stinker thought, "I presume there is some reason for not revealing my identity to your mother?"

"Sure. She's an adult."

"So?"

"Adults don't believe weird things very easily."

Once in Karen's room, her guest set about a thorough exploration. Drawers and boxes were opened and plowed through, the tape recorder was put through its paces, the pencil sharpener was twirled and then taken apart. All the while, Karen picked up little mental bursts of surprise, interest, amusement, and occasional disdain. She also realized that apparently a space explorer's training did not include putting things back as you found them. She hated to think what her mother would say if she came in now.

"Uh, Stinker, if you want to see the encyclopedia, it's over here. It's just a junior edition, of course, but . . . say, can you read?"

Stinker gave the mental equivalent of an indignant snort. "Of course. I picked that up out of your mind."

Karen raised startled hands to her head. That sneaky skunk's worse than a pickpocket, she thought.

Stinker looked up from the jewelbox he was examining, a plastic bangle dangling over one ear. "Sorry. Don't mean to offend you. I forget you're not used to working with your mind this way."

"Oh, that's okay. Take what you need, I guess. At least it doesn't hurt. I'll go down and fix us some peanut butter sandwiches."

When she returned with a plate of sandwiches and a couple of oranges, Karen found the skunk squatted in front of volume A of the encyclopedia, smoothly scanning a page, then turning it with his little furry paws.

She stopped in the doorway and stared. This more than anything else convinced her of Stinker's story. After all, talking animals were old hat—in fairy tales, at least. But *reading* animals . . .

She stepped into the room, quickly closing the door behind her. "Don't let my folks catch you doing that— or typing or turning on the TV. Take your cue from Sancho. He's probably about as stupid as your average skunk."

"Sancho? Is that what that type of animal is called?"

"No, he's a dog. Sancho's his name. They called him that because when I was little I couldn't say 'cocker spaniel.' It came out 'cockeyed Spaniard.' "

"Oh." He didn't get the allusion, and from a scan of Karen's mind, he could tell she wasn't too clear about it either. Something to do with a character in some large boring book.

The next day, when it was time for school, Karen left Stinker in her room with a bowl of peanuts, the last of the peanut butter cookies and several apples— the apples being an attempt at balancing his diet.

Before leaving to catch the bus, she took his picture with her father's Polaroid camera. She had wanted to take Stinker along in person to show the kids at school, but her parents had firmly said no. It would probably cause a riot, they thought, and Karen decided that fun as that might be, they were probably right. But at least she could flaunt the picture. Having an apparently pet skunk seemed to Karen a surefire way to raise her prestige at this new school.

On the bus coming home, Jonathan Waldron actually sat next to her and after a few awkward minutes asked to see the picture. He seemed genuinely impressed. Smugly Karen thought how impressed Jonathan would be if he knew the truth about this particular skunk. Let him keep his old spaceship models!

Back in her room again, Karen found Stinker just finishing volume U. The floor was littered with peanut shells and apple cores, and Sancho was flopped on a rug, soulful brown eyes fixed lovingly on his new friend.

She plunked down a stack of books onto her bed. "I took out some books on space travel from the school library. That encyclopedia's not very up to date for scientific stuff."

"Oh, glad to hear it," Stinker thought back at her. "I was beginning to wonder—though I've been learning a lot about the ancient city of Ur and also Ulysses and Ungulates." He got up, shook himself, and began waddling toward the bed.

"Not yet," she said firmly, placing a hand on the pile of books. "All work and no play makes a dull skunk, also maybe a dead one."

"Huh? But I don't want to play. My dignity. . . ."

"Never mind your dignity! As far as anyone can tell, you are a skunk. Dad took that ad to the paper this morning. In a few days, maybe a week, when nobody claims you, they'll want to take you to the pound—unless you've proven what a fine family pet you make."

Stinker picked up her mental image of the animal pound. "Right." He turned to Sancho. "Let's go play."

5

Despair of a Stranded Skunk

When Karen's father got out of his car that night, he was greeted by the sight of his daughter playing ball with a cocker spaniel and a skunk. He watched with amazement as the little black and white player continuously outwitted the flop-eared golden one.

"That's some animal," he said, shaking his head in grudging admiration, as he walked up to Karen. "I never would have guessed a skunk could make such a good pet. He's really quite bright. His owner ought to be eager to get him back. Just don't let him go wandering off, Karen. We don't want him bringing back any of his woodsy friends."

"Oh, don't worry, Dad. Stinker's a real home lover." As her father walked away, Karen continued to herself, "It's just that his home's some distance away."

When she turned back to the animals, she found Stinker and Sancho sitting side by side, vigorously scratching themselves with hind feet. The dog seemed resigned to it, but his companion was not.

"I don't think much of these little biting creatures that seem to have come with this body," Stinker thought at Karen. "I keep giving them mental commands to leave. They do, but they have apallingly short memories."

"I don't think fleas are known for their high intelligence," Karen replied. "Just don't scratch much in front of Mom and Dad. They'd make you wear a flea collar. Then you'd smell worse than a. . . ."

"Do stop making uncomplimentary references to odor."

Stinker also did not think much of the dog kibbles Karen's mother served him for dinner, although on the kitchen floor beside him, Sancho eagerly gobbled up his own bowlful. The skunk forced some down, however, after Karen sprinkled them with peanut butter morsels.

After dinner, he took a quick look at the new space flight books, then settled down in Karen's lap in the living room while the family watched a movie on television. It was a popular space saga with plenty of interstellar dogfights and blazing lasers. Stinker watched with excited intensity.

Karen's father noticed, "Look at that skunk, will you?" he laughed. "You'd almost think he was following the story."

"Oh, no," Karen protested quickly. "I'm sure he just likes the moving shapes, or maybe it's the food commercials." She felt an annoyed kick from a hairy paw.

After the movie when Stinker and Karen had gone upstairs, he shot a question at her. "How old are those books you brought back, anyway?"

"The space flight ones? Oh, pretty old, I guess. Ten years, maybe."

"Only that old? Then how could you people have moved in a few years from the primitive stuff in the books to what we were watching tonight?"

"Oh, that was just a story. It's made up."

"A story! But . . . what about all that other stuff you know about? The Dark Destroyer, the Princess of Light?"

"They're just stories, too. But, heck, if I hadn't been into that sort of thing I'd probably never have believed *you* so easily."

His mental groan went to Karen's heart. Suddenly understanding, she knelt down beside him. "You mean, you thought. . . ."

His bushy tail drooped. "I mean, this might not have been the best planet to crash land on."

When Karen came home from school the next day, she found Stinker pacing back and forth across her room. "It's hopeless!" he thought at her. "These books make it clear. I'd have as good a chance of getting home from here if I sprouted wings and tried to fly."

She sat down and scooped the dejected animal into her lap. With one hand she scratched the white patch on his head, while the other traced the pattern along his back. Despite himself Stinker purred, rubbing against her fingers.

"You know," she said, "you're welcome to stay here if my parents say it's okay."

"Thanks," he answered dully. "I mean, I appreciate the sentiment, but I simply can't stay here. Sylon High Command must receive the information I have about the Zarnk attack."

After a moment the skunk got up from Karen's lap, ruffled his long silky fur, and with determination padded toward the door. "I guess I should go back and take another look at that wreck. Maybe there is something I can do with it after all."

Soon with Sancho trotting eagerly behind, they slipped out the back door and headed off to the woods.

In his former body, Stinker realized, he'd probably have had trouble finding the crash site again, but this one led them right to it. The land here was so boggy that already the landing scar and even the wreckage of the ship were disappearing under mud and watery green scum.

He felt slightly squeamish about confronting the remains of his former body—he had been very attached to it—but he found that the forest scavengers had rather thoroughly removed all traces. Indignantly, he wished indigestion on them. He did not care for the thought of having been somebody's dinner, not at any stage.

Karen sat on a fallen log and watched as Stinker scrambled over the remains of his ship, digging here and there, Sancho enthusiastically helping.

From what Karen could see sticking above the surface, this might almost be another old rusted car that had been dumped in the woods. For an interstellar adventurer, she decided, this fellow seemed awfully low profile: a peanut-guzzling skunk who arrived in a broken-down jalopy. Oh well, maybe he cuts a more impressive figure in his own setting.

He looked far from impressive when he finally came back to the log, bedraggled and covered with mud. He crawled up beside Karen, his tail drooping dejectedly over the side. Irrepressibly cheerful, Sancho sat at Karen's feet, panting and thumping his short tail against the ground.

Stinker sighed. "It seems the drive unit is pretty well intact, but the ship itself is a total write-off. Those mass-produced scout ships ought to be banned from the market. At home I have a trim little one-person fighter that could have taken a landing like that with hardly a scratch." He sighed again and began picking absently at the rotten bark. Without thinking, he popped a grub into his mouth.

"Well, if the engine still runs," Karen said, trying to ignore the grub, "maybe you could build a new ship."

"With the technology you have on this backward rock? Ha! You might as well ask those ancient people of Ur to build an automobile."

Karen bristled at the slur to her planet but had to

admit, after some reflection, that he was probably right. "It's getting late," she said, standing up. "We'd better head back. You may have see-in-the-dark eyes, but I haven't."

The woods were cold and purpling with coming night when the three stepped from their shadows. High above, the last rays of sun were lighting a vapor trail as it etched a white line across the deep blue sky.

"What about putting your engine in an airplane?" Karen suggested suddenly.

"Too flimsy," came the dejected reply. "Even the best wouldn't last more than a few minutes outside the atmosphere."

As they approached home, Stinker's head hung low and his muddy tail dragged listlessly along the ground. Karen had never seen an animal look so depressed.

"Hey, you'd better perk up, or my mother will want to take you to the vet."

Stinker got a mental picture of shots and pills and having thermometers stuck up his hind-end—and quickly his head and tail rose jauntily into the air.

As they walked in the front door, they could hear the drone of television. Picking up Stinker, she settled onto the couch beside her father's recliner. The evening news was on with its usual display of maps, film clips, and serious, neatly groomed announcers.

Sitting listlessly in Karen's lap, Stinker paid little attention until suddenly his little ears swiveled around like radar. On the screen an announcer talked about a space shuttle flight to take place in two weeks. Stinker's beady black eyes sparkled, and he squirmed about in Karen's lap.

Her father looked over. "Has that creature got fleas?"

"Oh, no. It's . . . it's just that skunks in the wild are nocturnal animals. He still gets kind of antsy at sunset." Karen had been reading the encyclopedia too. With the excited skunk tucked awkwardly under one arm, Karen stood up, "Guess I'll go wash for dinner."

"Can't you hold still?" she thought at Stinker when she'd reached the top of the stairs.

"Well, put me down then. I've got feet! Why wasn't that ship written up in those space books?"

"Oh, I guess it was only in the planning stages when they were written. But why? All it does is orbit a few times and land again."

"But it was designed for space travel! Where it goes depends on the propulsion system—and the pilot."

"Maybe, but. . . . Hey, what do you have in mind, anyway?"

"It's obvious. We have to hijack the space shuttle."

6

An Alliance Expanded

Quickly Karen shut her bedroom door behind them. "You're crazy! They launch those things down in Florida, behind lots of fences, with lots of guards around. They're not about to let some skunk march up and take over the ship."

Stinker sat down, resting his chin on crossed paws. "Hmm, that *does* pose difficulties—the security arrangements, I mean. Obviously we'll have to bring it down somewhere close, where there's no one to guard it."

"What?"

"Those flat fields up the road should do."

"You want to make the space shuttle land in the Waldrons' soybean fields?"

"Yes, that would be fine. Then we wouldn't have to drag my drive unit very far."

"I don't like the way you keep thinking 'we.' "

Stinker's whiskers drooped and his black eyes looked pathetic. "But of course I'll need your help. I don't know very much about this space shuttle of yours."

"It isn't mine! It belongs to a bunch of scientists. And anyway, I don't know the first thing about it. I'm not like nerdy Jonathan."

"Oh. Who is this Jonathan? A friend of yours?"

"Not a friend! No . . . an acquaintance."

"Well then, let's go ask him about the shuttle."

"I can't!"

"Why not? Does he live very far from here?"

"No, he lives just up the road. But I can't go up there and talk with him."

"Why not?"

"He's a boy!"

Stinker was silent a moment. "I was not aware that males of your species were mute. Your father certainly is not."

"No, no, it's just that . . . Oh, all right, all right. We'll go talk with him. But I wouldn't do this for just any skunk!"

With one excuse or another, Karen managed to put off the ordeal until Saturday, but at last she could delay no longer.

The day was gray and overcast, like her mood. After breakfast, she trudged up the road with Stinker trotting jauntily behind. As they approached the large gray farmhouse, Karen felt it looked more like a forbidding medieval fortress or some wizard's lair in an alternate universe.

With heavy hand, she knocked on the front door, desperately hoping the entire family was out, but to her despair, a woman opened the door and smiled inquiringly.

"Good morning, Mrs. Waldron. Uh . . . the other day Jonathan said he was interested in seeing my pet skunk, and . . . and so I've brought him over."

"Oh . . . yes." The smile wavered and Mrs. Waldron took an involuntary step back.

"Oh, don't worry. He's deodorized and very friendly."

"Yes. Yes, certainly. Jonathan did talk about him. I'm sure he'll be delighted. I'll go tell him you're here." Hastily she disappeared from the doorway, leaving Karen to stand brooding on the porch.

Stinker thought at her, "I don't understand, Karen. If this person is your age, your neighbor, and your schoolmate, why aren't you friends?"

She groaned. "Social customs far too complex for you to understand."

From upstairs came the sound of Jonathan's mother knocking on a door, and then a muffled "Yes?"

Blushing guiltily, Karen took a step inside to hear better. "Karen from down the road is here to see you, Jonathan."

"What? She's a girl! Tell her I'm sick or something."

"I know she's a girl, silly. It wouldn't kill you to talk with one. Besides, she's brought that pet skunk you were going on about."

Silence. Then, "Well, all right. Send her up."

"Yes, your lordship. 'Send her up,' indeed."

Hastily Karen stepped back, but she felt better. She had something Jonathan wanted. And it seemed he didn't like to be with girls any more than she did with boys. Well, they'd just have to endure each other for the sake of the universe.

Keeping a cautious distance, Mrs. Waldron ushered Karen and Stinker up the stairs and through the door.

As she stepped into the room, Karen looked around curiously. Hanging by transparent threads from the ceiling was a fleet of plastic spacecraft. Not all were Russian or American models. There were a fair sprinkling of Klingon and Romulan battle cruisers, Imperial fighters and other fantastic craft. Walls not lined with bookshelves were covered with posters. Prosaic sky charts and NASA publicity posters mixed with cinemagraphic heroes and villains brandishing weapons. On one table sat Jonathan's ham radio set she'd heard about, and on the other was the terminal for a home computer.

Then her eyes fell on Jonathan, who sat slumped down behind a desk strewn with pieces of a half-finished model of a space fighter. Sunlight from the window glinted off his glasses. "Well?" he said coldly.

He sounds just like Ming the Merciless giving audience, Karen thought. "Uh . . . hello, Jonathan. I sort of thought you'd like to meet my pet skunk."

On cue, Stinker waddled out from behind her and began exploring the room. With nothing to say to each other, Karen and Jonathan concentrated on watching the skunk.

Bookcases were examined, drawers opened, and the

radio given thorough scrutiny. When Stinker's inquisitive paws began twirling a black globe dotted with pin-sized holes, Karen couldn't help asking, "What's that?"

"That," said Jonathan in a grand tone, "is my planetarium. I'll show you." Now honestly eager, he jumped up, pulled down the window shades, and flipped a switch on the base of the globe. Suddenly the darkened room was transformed into a starry sky. Tiny pinpricks of light shone on the walls and ceiling in rough semblance of constellations.

"See, there's Orion and Taurus and the Pleiades." He went on to point out the other constellations, distorted somewhat as they bent around corners or splayed over furniture. Finally opening the shades, he sat down again. "Pretty neat, huh?"

"Primitive but effective," came an answer. "A little too schematic and two-dimensional to be useful for navigation, though."

"Well, of course. . . ." Jonathan stopped awkwardly. "Karen, did you say something just now?"

"She didn't, but I did," another answered inside his mind.

Jonathan clapped both hands to his head. Suddenly the skunk jumped on his lap and, planting both front paws firmly on his chest, looked him in the face.

"It's me, Tsynq Yr, operative of the Sylon Confederacy."

Jonathan's voice was on the high edge of hysteria. "Karen, are you some sort of weird ventriloquist?"

To her surprise, Karen suddenly felt sorry for him.

• 35 •

"Hey, Stinker, don't come on so strong," she said aloud. "You're a little hard to take all at once, you know."

"Sorry," the skunk thought in reply as he settled more sedately into Jonathan's lap. "Explain as you see fit."

Karen did, with Stinker throwing in an occasional supplementary thought. Afterwards, Jonathan looked across at Karen, trying to avoid seeing the skunk who was now on his desk busily assembling pieces of his model.

"And I'm supposed to believe that?"

Karen got up from the edge of the table where she'd been sitting. "Well, isn't it better than believing in a mind-melding skunk who could probably beat you in computer games?"

He looked down at the busy little black paws. "Yes, I guess it is." He was silent a minute. "But what I really can't believe is that I'd be of any use in trying to hijack the space shuttle. I mean, that's really crazy!"

"Ah, but what I need first is information," Stinker thought at him as he slotted the plastic space pilot into the cockpit. "I need to learn everything I can about the shuttle's design and operation. Engine plans, reentry procedures, that sort of thing."

Karen snorted, thinking it unlikely that her neighbor could supply anything of the sort. But Jonathan, regaining some of his composure, shot her a superior glare.

"Sure, I've got most of that. If a kid writes a sincere enough letter, the NASA public relations people'll send most anything."

Jonathan rummaged through drawers and shelves and

stacks of papers until he had built a considerable pile of booklets and brochures on the floor by his desk. Stinker, who was having difficulties with the little tube of glue, happily abandoned the model and climbed down. He began spreading the material over the rug, turning pages, examining diagrams, occasionally emitting little squeals and grunts of satisfaction.

The other two watched in awkward silence until there came a sudden knock at the door. "Can I get you kids something to eat?" Mrs. Waldron's voice said. "It's lunchtime."

Jonathan jumped up and hurled himself against the door. He didn't care to explain the studiously reading skunk, should his mother come in. "Oh yeah, great idea, Mom. Thanks. How about some sandwiches?"

"Make them peanut butter," came an unvoiced addition. On the other side of the door, Mrs. Waldron shook her head and went down to make peanut butter sandwiches.

When the last sandwich had been eaten, Stinker began thinking at them excitedly while using his tail to wipe off the peanut butter he'd smeared over the cover of *The Child's First Book of the Space Shuttle*.

"I believe I can do it. Some more detailed plans would be useful, of course. These things are awfully schematic. But I do think it can be done. I'll need your help for the next stage, though."

"Wait a minute, Stinky. . . ."

"Tsynq Yr, if you please."

"All right, all right, Stinker. Showing you kiddies' books and NASA PR stuff is one thing. But I'm not sure I want to help you storm the launchpad, firing lasers or whatever, and take over the shuttle. I mean, they've got lots of soldiers and everything around there. And machine guns, I bet."

"Oh, well, I actually hadn't planned anything as adventurous as that. Are you disappointed?"

"Disappointed?" Karen said. "Hardly. It's just that . . . well, it's just that stealing valuable U.S. Government property for a pet skunk. . . ."

"Pet skunk!" came the injured reply. "I thought we were friends. I mean, even if you two can't manage to be friends with each other, you can both be with me, can't you?"

"Oh sure, but. . . ."

"So what are friends for? They're to help each other. Right?"

"Sure but. . . ."

"So I'll help you both to have a small, relatively safe adventure, and you help me get off the planet. And don't worry about the U.S. Government. I can see that their property's returned when I'm through with it."

"Well. . . ."

Stinker jumped up and waddled toward the door. "Now the first thing I need to do is dig that power unit out of my ship before it sinks any farther into the ooze."

"Sure," Jonathan said resignedly as he reached for his jacket, "what are friends for?"

7

Baddies at One's Doorstep

They stopped at the Waldrons' barn for a couple of shovels, then continued down the road to Karen's house. In the dilapidated gardening shed they clattered about, moving rakes and hoes until they pulled free an old red wagon. After a moment's thought, Karen hurried to the kitchen door and stuck her head in.

"I'm off to play in the woods, Mom. Already had lunch."

Her mother peered through the window above the sink. "Oh, you have Jonathan with you. How nice."

Karen's stomach churned at the sight of her mother's pleased smile. She stalked away. The sacrifices one had to make for interstellar adventure!

Karen and Jonathan took turns hauling the wagon. It rattled and wobbled behind them as the three set out toward the woods. Some of the leaves had fallen in the previous day's rain and now lay in a sodden carpet underfoot. Other trees still blazed their leaves against the lead gray sky. Brave torches against the encroaching power of darkness, Karen thought, shivering. The woods didn't look nearly so friendly today.

Unerringly they made their way to the crash site. As forest mingled with bog, the air smelled of damp earth and rotting vegetation. Their wagon bumped noisily over roots and fallen branches. The silence they disturbed had a waiting menace about it.

At first Jonathan was disappointed with the ship itself, but as he poked and prodded among the exposed remains, he became more impressed. "This sure is weird-feeling metal."

"No-good cheap stuff," was Stinker's reply. "My own Sylon fighter would never have broken up like this."

"I don't understand why nobody saw the crash," Jonathan said as he fingered an odd fragment of machinery.

Karen answered. "It was really stormy that night, remember? What with all the lightning, a falling spaceship or two would never have been noticed."

With the children wielding shovels and Stinker alternately directing them and scrabbling with his paws, they slowly cleared away part of the wreck. After a while, among twisted metal shards, they began exposing a smooth metallic cylinder elaborated with numerous odd projections.

"Is that what we're looking for?" Jonathan said, pushing sweaty hair out from behind his glasses. "It looks in pretty good shape."

"Yes. These units, at least, are made to last—even when they're put in a piece of space junk like this ship."

Struggling and heaving, the three managed to drag the thing out of the ground and into the wagon. The wheels sank into the muck with wet sucking sounds until they finally hauled it onto stony ground. Then, damp with sweat and mud, they sat down wearily on a mossy hummock to catch their breath.

A few birds chirped halfheartedly in the gray woods. Otherwise the only sound was the dripping of foggy dampness from tree branches and a faint rattling, like wind-stirred reeds.

Suddenly Stinker stiffened, his fur bristling like a porcupine's. "Did you hear that?"

"What?" Jonathan said. "The birds, the wind?"

"That rattling. Hurry, we've got to get out of here!" The little animal scurried over to the wagon. "Come on! I can't pull this by myself."

Catching his fear, though not knowing why, Jonathan and Karen jumped up and joined him.

"But I don't get it," Karen said as she pushed the balky wagon while Jonathan pulled. "What's the hurry?" Slowly their charge creaked forward with its heavy load.

"That noise! It's them! They've found me."

"Who?"

The rattling noise was suddenly closer, sounding like

wind chimes made from dried bones. Stinker's thoughts hissed like a snake. "The Zarnk!"

There was a sudden movement in the grayness to their left. Karen and Jonathan spun around to see something emerging from bushes twenty feet away. It looked like a loose collection of bamboo poles held together at the top by a huge glob of amber glue.

The thing clattered forward. It stopped and slowly raised one pole-like appendage. Something metallic glinted at its end.

"It's armed, run!" squeaked a mental order. And the two children ran. Stinker bolted after them, but after a few bounds he suddenly stopped and reared up on his hind legs.

Karen, seeing this out of the corner of her eye, gasped and skidded to a halt. "Oh, no! His skunk instincts are taking over!"

Stinker thrust his tail into the air, aimed at the advancing enemy, and sprayed. A cloud of oily stench shot toward the thing.

The creature continued forward. Suddenly it stopped, swayed, and shrieked like a bagpipe. The gelatinous mass at its top began to solidify and crack. Blindly the thing staggered back and forth, its top disintegrating into powdery shards. The shrieking died hollowly away, and the pole legs clattered to the ground.

"Wow!" Jonathan blurted out. His legs were suddenly trembling as they staggered back toward Stinker. "I guess those Zarnk guys are allergic to skunk spray."

Karen was shivering, wishing she hadn't seen what she just had. That was nightmare material, for sure. She shook her head. "Some allergy! All I've ever had is a rash from eating shellfish."

Stinker was silent, his nose twitching as he gazed at his fallen enemy. "I can't believe it," he muttered mentally. "That Zarnk nearly shot me. I wanted to run, and this idiotic body made me do that instead. I've never seen that happen to a Zarnk before."

"First class chemical warfare," Jonathan said, trying to sound calm through chattering teeth.

"It certainly was," the skunk answered thoughtfully.

"Uh, Stinker," Karen ventured, "are there likely to be any more of those things about?"

"Huh? Oh, no, not likely. He was probably a lone scout sent to follow my trail. But we'd better get moving. If he got some sort of message off, they might investigate sooner or later."

With renewed commitment, they hauled the wagon out of the woods and aimed their procession toward Karen's house. "We can hide this thing in the gardening shed," she suggested. "My mom won't be pottering around in there again until spring."

After dragging the wagon into the cramped, musty-smelling shed, they stuffed it into a corner, then covered it with half-filled bags of mulch. For added effect, they stacked some rakes, hoes, and trellises against it. Finally they stepped back out into the gray daylight, and Karen firmly shut the shed door.

She wished she could shut her mind as firmly against the memories of that thing in the woods. Here was space adventure at her doorstep, but somehow it wasn't as clean and exciting as maybe meeting the Dark Destroyer or the Princess of Light. It was downright scary.

8

The Best Laid Plans . . .

During the next week, Karen and her skunk were regular afterschool visitors at Jonathan's house. Both mothers acted insufferably pleased, much to their children's annoyance. Theirs was, as Jonathan said pointedly, "purely a business relationship in support of a mutual friend."

Stinker soon turned from examining the shuttle information to tearing apart the ham radio. At first this put Jonathan in a dither, but the little skunk did seem to know what he was doing. When handling human-designed tools for a job proved too difficult, he'd use his sharp little claws.

"But I really don't understand," Jonathan had said early on, "how this is going to help. I mean, ham radios don't pick up NASA—not the secret important stuff, anyway."

"Ah yes, but it's wonderful what a little tinkering can do, particularly when I can link things up with your home computer here. It is incredibly primitive, but it does what we need, just the same."

"And exactly what do we need?" Karen asked.

"We need to change the reentry programming and bring the shuttle down in that field out there."

Karen looked out the window, pulling aside the curtains with their red and blue rocket-ship design. Jonathan followed her gaze, a frown wrinkling his forehead.

"I hate to be a spoilsport, but I don't think the shuttle can land on a soybean field. It's too uneven, too many ruts. The landing gear is pretty much like an ordinary airplane's, you know."

"You mean your airplanes can't land on a flat surface like that?"

"Well, there aren't any huge bumps, but it's hardly flat, not smooth anyway. That's why planes need paved runways or dry lakebeds or something, so they don't flip over while they're landing."

Stinker thought something that did not translate. Then he clambered up on the window sill and glowered out. "All right. Next assignment, team. I'll look up the width of the shuttle's axle, and you two go down and measure the width of that road."

"The road!" Karen exclaimed.

"Why not? It's straight for a long distance. Quite long enough, I think."

Jonathan looked at Karen, sighed, then went to his

closet and fetched a yardstick that carried the legend "Time Measures All Things," courtesy of a funeral home. Soon the two were headed outside.

The road never carried much traffic, so it wasn't long before they felt safe getting down on hands and knees and measuring the width of the pavement and the hard gravelly shoulder.

"This is crazy, you know," Jonathan muttered as he scuttled like a crab over the asphalt.

"Yeah, particularly since this whole thing is probably going to fail."

"Good thing, too."

Karen looked at him. "You mean you don't want him to succeed? Then why . . . ?"

"Oh, I *want* him to. That'd be best, sure. But have you thought about what happens to accomplices of folks who hijack space shuttles?"

She swallowed hard. "Well, no. No one's ever done it before."

"Then we may be the first to find out."

Steadily the date drew nearer for the proposed launch of the shuttle. Karen and her furry companion regularly watched the evening news for any references to it. Her father commented on her commendable new interest in public affairs, which she hastily attributed to her current events unit at school.

One night after the news, while the family was eating dinner, a large expensive-looking car rolled up their gravel drive. Through their dining room window they saw a middle-aged woman with a great beehive of hair get out of the car and walk importantly toward their door.

Karen's mother answered as soon as the doorbell rang, and the strange woman gushed in. "Hello, hello. I am Mrs. Van Voorhis. I should have phoned I know, but I couldn't wait. I wanted to come right away and surprise everyone."

"Uh . . . yes," Karen's mother said. "But about what?"

"It's your ad in the paper. I've come to retrieve my dear little Flower."

"Flower?"

"The skunk, my dear. You advertised that you found my pet skunk."

Karen suddenly jumped up from the table. "Oh, but Stinker can't be yours!"

"Stinker indeed!" Then she smiled. "But yes, he must be mine. I lost my little Flower while passing through your town last spring when we were driving back from Florida. My sister-in-law chanced upon your ad in the paper and sent it on to me. The skunk you found must be mine, dear. Tame skunks aren't very common, you know."

"Maybe not, but this one isn't yours."

"You can't be sure of that, Karen," her mother said. "He very well might be."

In the kitchen where Stinker had been eating with Sancho, he'd picked up Karen's alarm. Now he had pushed his way through the swinging door and was making like a furtive shadow along the wall toward the stairs.

But Mrs. Van Voorhis caught a glimpse of black and white. "Ah, there he is now, my sweet little Flower. Come to Mama, Sweetkins!"

Stinker darted for the open door. As the creature dashed between his legs, Karen's father reached down and grabbed him around the middle. Stinker squirmed and thrashed but was held firm. "Quick, Helen, get me something to put him in!"

Karen's mother looked around frantically. Running into the living room, she dumped out some books they'd been boxing for a rummage sale and hurried back with the box.

Squealing "No, no!" Karen tried to grab Stinker away, but her father managed to cram the squirming animal into the box and jam down the lid.

"Here," he said, handing the box to the woman, his lips a tight angry line. "It would have been better if you'd called first. We've all become rather attached to him, I'm afraid. But I'm sure Stink . . . Flower will be happy with his rightful owner again."

Awkwardly the woman took the box as it thumped and jumped from inside. "Yes, I understand. He's such a little sweetypie, I can see how he'd win anyone's heart. And I am so grateful for you taking care of him all this time. Isn't there something I can. . . ."

"No, no. I think you'd better just go now. Good-bye, Mrs. Van Voorhis."

The door closed and Karen burst into tears. "Oh, Daddy, how could you?"

"Karen," he said firmly. "I liked him, too. But he

was her skunk. To keep him, once we knew that, would have been theft."

"But we *didn't* know that. Skunks do look a lot alike, but he wasn't her skunk!"

"He had to be. She was right: tame skunks are not very common. And she lost hers right around here. It'd be too much of a coincidence to have two skunks like him in the area."

Karen stared at her father. "Oh, you don't understand!" she wailed, then turned and ran up the stairs. She slammed her bedroom door behind her. No, she thought miserably, you won't find two skunks like that very easily. Not two stranded skunks from outer space.

9

A Missing Conspirator

Karen found the next few days nearly unbearable. For a while she thought that if Stinker could just get to a phone, he'd call, and she and Jonathan could set up a rescue. But then she realized that was silly. After all, he couldn't talk, not out loud, and she imagined one couldn't just think over a telephone.

Finally the day of the shuttle launch arrived. Earlier, Karen had planned to play sick so she could stay home from school and watch it. Now she couldn't wait to get away from the house and the morning radio's chatter about the upcoming launch.

Grimly she stood by the roadside in front of her house waiting for the school bus. She looked up as Jonathan plodded dejectedly down the road to join her.

"No word, I take it," he said flatly.

"None."

"I don't get it. I mean, surely he could have gotten away from that woman by now. She wouldn't know she was dealing with more than your average skunk intelligence."

"Yeah, but in the meantime, she could have driven three states away. I don't guess it's very easy for unescorted skunks to travel long distances. He couldn't just hop a Greyhound."

They were silent a moment. Karen thought about skunks trudging along highways and about all the dead skunks you always see in the middle of roads. "And think of the dangers of traveling that far. Cars and dogs and. . . ."

"And Zarnk."

"Oh, no!" she exclaimed. "You think there could be more of them?"

"Stinker said there was a chance that the one fellow could have gotten off a message. And later when he looked and couldn't find that Zarnk's ship, he said it could have been programmed to go into orbit after a certain time and act as a beacon."

Karen shivered at the thought of a Zarnk hit squad clattering about. She was actually relieved when the bus came and took them off to the comforting normality of school.

In the afternoon, the school bus dropped her off at home just as the mail truck was pulling away. Her mother was already out at the box sorting through the mail.

"Bills, ads, and bank statements. Dull, dull. Here's something for you, Karen. My word, it looks as if it's been dragged through the gutter. You'd think the postal service would take better care of things."

She handed Karen a pictureless prestamped postcard. It was creased down the middle and blotted with a coffee stain. On one side an address was written and just as neatly crossed out in ink, while beside it in stubby pencil her own name and address was written in a clumsy childish hand. Perplexed, she flipped the card over and scanned the penciled message. Her heart leaped.

"Karen: Escaped crazy lady. Have important errand. Will be back in time. Please lay in big stock of peanuts, peanut butter, etc. Your friend, S."

She whooped with delight and ran up the road to show Jonathan. She found him in his kitchen, putting together an afterschool snack.

He read the card and his normally solemn face bloomed into smiles. "Boy, it looks like he pulled this out of some garbage can. Must have rooted around for hours before he found something he could reuse. Guess he figured most post offices wouldn't sell stamps to a skunk."

"I wonder what his important errand is."

"I don't know, but he'd better come back soon. He's monkeyed with my radio so much, I'm afraid to touch it. I might disintegrate myself or something."

Karen was about to chide him for caring more about

his old radio than their friend. But she stopped. Clearly Jonathan was very happy to hear that Stinker was all right.

"Well," she said after a minute, "at least we can get on the provisioning detail. Maybe instead of catching the bus after school we should go stock up at the grocery store and walk home."

Jonathan groaned at the thought of the long walk. "Yeah, I guess we'll have to. Can't exactly ask our mothers to pick up a crate of peanut butter next time they're at the store—not without a few questions. Do you suppose real skunks like the stuff as much as space skunks?"

"Probably. I think skunks like everything. But let's lay in some lettuce or something else too, so he doesn't get scurvy."

The next day they told their parents they'd be late getting home from school. It was nearly dusk when they finally staggered up the road from town, grocery bags bulging with peanuts, peanut butter, peanut butter cookies, and bags of dried apples. Allowance hoards had been severely depleted, and all the way back Jonathan had grumbled about the unlikelihood of getting repaid by the Sylon government.

At last, slipping into the gardening shed they hid the provisions with the alien engine under bags of mulch and potting soil.

The next few days were passed in anxious waiting. Homework suffered, but neither Karen nor Jonathan missed a word that TV or radio had to say about the ongoing shuttle flight. They knew who was spacewalking outside the ship and testing what pieces of equipment. They knew the family background of every astronaut, which scientific tests were successful and which firmly refused to work, and they knew what the crew ate and who got most severely space sick.

Karen went to bed with technical terms buzzing around in her head: extravehicular activity, O-ring seals, solid fuel boosters, manned maneuvering units. She knew the shuttle was orbiting 185 miles up at a speed of some 17,270 miles per hour. She never used to have any interest in these details but now found them surprisingly compelling. Even the Princess of Light, she grudging admitted, had to know how her flittership worked when she set off on some space adventure.

As the days of the mission passed by with no sign of Stinker, Karen and Jonathan became worried again. One news item on a local station caught Karen's interest for a moment because it dealt with skunks. State police several counties to their north had reported an unusual migration of skunks, a black and white wave pouring across the highway like lemmings marching to the sea. The announcer treated it like a joke, quipping that they'd have to add Skunk Alert to other things like Tornado Warning and Winter Storm Watch.

It was interesting enough, but Karen didn't see how it could have anything to do with Stinker. She just hoped that farmers didn't get so upset at the thought of hordes of skunks that they'd shoot one on sight. As the days passed she kept worrying more and more about farmers with guns, and dogs, and cars, and . . . even Zarnk. It didn't help her sleep any.

The day before the shuttle was scheduled to land, Karen and Jonathan avoided each other on the bus and at school. Both of them almost believed that their adventure and possibly their friend had come to an end. But somehow it seemed that if they didn't speak these words it wouldn't be true. That night Karen ate very little and went to bed early, causing her mother to worry that she was ill.

She dreamed that Mr. Spock of the Starship Enterprise was teamed up with the Princess of Light, who looked remarkably like the teacher Karen had had back in second grade. Hiding on a garbage truck, they were trying to escape from samurai warriors whose main weapon seemed to be bamboo wind chimes that they shook threateningly. Mr. Spock, who, to nobody's apparent surprise, had sprouted a skunk tail, was trying to construct a grenade out of empty peanut butter jars, when suddenly one of the wind chimes came alive and started loping down the road after their slowly escaping garbage truck. The Princess of Light desperately hurled peanut shells at it.

Shivering and sweaty, Karen woke up. She could still hear the clatter of peanut shells against bamboo. The sound outlasted the wisps of dream.

She sat up and stared fearfully at her window. Outside

in the dark, one branch seemed to be bobbing up and down, tapping rhythmically against the glass pane. A dark lump squatted on the branch, and from it came the glint of eyes.

10

Unscheduled Stop

Karen was at the window in one leap. Struggling with the latch, she slid up the lower half of the window. The dark lump moved awkwardly down the branch, almost falling onto the window sill.

A thought buzzed in her head. "Remember reading in the encyclopedia that skunks are not natural climbers? Let me tell you, they were right. Whew!" Stinker belly-flopped to the floor as his quivering little legs gave out totally.

Instantly, Karen scooped him into her lap and stroked his matted, brier-studded fur. "Oh, Stinker, I'm so glad to see you. We thought that dogs or Zarnk had got you."

"Zarnk? You haven't seen any of them, have you?"

"No, but I have an overactive imagination when it comes to disasters."

"Ah, yes. Well, there's no time for imagination or explanations now, I'm afraid. Skunk legs are maddeningly short; things took much longer than I'd planned. The shuttle will be breaking orbit soon. I've got to get to Jonathan's, and I need your help."

"Sure. What can I do?"

"Well, I can't just go knock on his door in the middle of the night. And there's no tree by his bedroom window—not that I would *ever* try that again. I was thinking of throwing something against his window so he'd come down and let me in. But skunks, I've discovered, have pretty poor aim."

"I can do that for you at least. Let me put on some clothes first, though. I don't have your lovely fur coat for prancing about in the cold. Oh, Stinker, I'm so glad you're safe!" She hugged the skunk and hurried to get dressed.

It took a number of pebbles against the window to wake their confederate. Karen thought that this sort of thing seemed to work a lot better in the movies. But finally Jonathan's tousled head appeared at the window. In the pale haze of moonlight, Karen pointed at Stinker and then at the door.

The head disappeared. In a minute there was a faint click and the kitchen door swung open. Karen and Stinker slipped in beside Jonathan, and the three scuttled up the stairs to his room.

Once the door was closed and the light switched on, Stinker took a brief look around the room. "Excellent, everything just as I left it. Now, I'd better get to work."

He scrambled onto the table that carried the now modified ham radio and computer. "Uh, Jonathan, you wouldn't happen to have any peanut butter cookies about, would you? I've been eating nothing but grubs, worms, and people's garbage for days."

Jonathan rummaged around in a drawer. "How about Chocolate Peanut Nuggets?"

"Lovely."

As Stinker chewed, he thought at Karen, "Now, you'd better get back home, young lady. You don't want people to talk."

"Don't be rude!" she shot back. But she admitted, the last thing she wanted was to be caught in a boy's bedroom at night.

"What do you need me to do there?"

"Nothing. Just go back to bed. Get up at the regular time and get ready for school as usual."

"What! You expect me to go off to school and miss all the fun?"

"Hey no, calm down. I just want you to act like normal. Go out and wait for the bus with Jonathan. Trust me. I won't let you miss any adventure."

Still disgruntled, Karen slipped quietly out of the room and down the stairs. She let herself out of the house and sped like a shadow down the road to her own home. All right, she'd trust him. But he'd sure better not let her miss anything. And she certainly didn't know how that bossy skunk expected her to get any more sleep.

The alarm woke her. She lay in bed a moment, surprised that she was already dressed. Then she remembered. Jumping up, she ran a brush through her hair and hurried downstairs.

"My, you're ready early," her mother said as she tended the bacon.

"Umm. Well, it's sort of a get-up-and-do kind of day."

Her father came in, and as part of the morning ritual switched on the radio. ". . . no explanation, but the NASA spokesman repeated that the shuttle reentry is not going as programmed. The orbital maneuvering engines fired at the wrong time. The shuttle remains in the correct reentry posture, but its present position may not allow it to land where planned. Attempts to abort the reentry apparently have failed. But NASA spokesmen stress that at present there is no danger to the crew."

Karen just sat and stared at the radio. Then guiltily she poured cereal into her bowl and began eating it, forgetting to pour on the milk.

"Those computers!" her father said as he poured his own cereal. "Once they get it in their heads to do something, there's no stopping them. I hope those hot-shot scientists had the sense to put in some manual controls as well or the thing may land in Russia or the ocean."

"Oh my, let's hope not," her mother said as she served up the bacon. "Karen dear, don't you want any milk on your cereal?"

"Oh." Karen suddenly choked on the dry flakes. "No, it's . . . too fattening."

Her mother gave her a knowing smile. "Little miss, suddenly worried about her figure."

Normally Karen would have bristled at that remark. Now she barely noted it as she reached to turn up the radio. ". . . reports that all attempts at manual override have failed. The shuttle continues to stick to an unprogrammed flight plan. And now it seems that radio contact with the crew has been lost."

Somehow Karen got through breakfast. The radio news switched to other items, repeatedly coming back to the out-of-control shuttle. Only with the greatest reluctance did she finally don her backpack and trudge out to the road. Maybe she could hop off at the next busstop and run back.

Jonathan was already there looking tense and tired. When she came up he whispered, "After you left last night, Stinker had me move all that stuff from the shed and hide it in that clump of willows beside the road there. I wish he wasn't so concerned about your 'reputation.' I could have used some help."

"Yeah, I think his view of Earth customs is a little dated. I let him watch too many old movies on television."

They were silent a while. One car whizzed past them stirring up an eddy of dry leaves. Dawn was turning the sky into a huge shell of Easter egg pink. From habit, they watched the long gray stretch of road. Finally they saw the distant blot of the approaching school bus.

"I don't know about you," Karen said quietly, "but I don't want to get on that bus."

"I know," Jonathan muttered. "Stinker said to trust him but, I mean. . . ." Suddenly he broke off. In the sky above the school bus another blot could be seen. It glinted silver.

"Holy cow," he said. "Look at that! It's the shuttle!"

Karen stared entranced as the silver speck took shape: wings and a pointed beak like a great metallic bird. It hurtled toward them, lower and lower along the line of road. The distant bus came to a screeching halt as the driver noticed the competition directly overhead.

A window-shaking roar filled the sky. Both Karen's and Jonathan's parents ran out of their houses as the graceful spacecraft touched down, its landing wheels rolling neatly along the hard shoulder of the road.

Over the noise, two sets of parents called for their children to run, but fascinated by the sight, Karen and Jonathan stayed put. Hadn't their friend said to trust him? With a dying roar, the ship slowed to a halt on the stretch of road between the two farmhouses, right beside an innocent-looking clump of willows.

11

Chaos on the Farm

For a long moment, silence hung heavily in the air. Then the watchers began talking among themselves and slowly walking toward the huge out-of-place vehicle.

After several minutes, a metallic click came from the side of the ship, and the hatch slowly opened. Cautiously a man in a flight suit peered out.

"Uh, good morning. Madam, may I use your telephone?"

From then on the day progressed in steadily increasing pandemonium. With no rolling airport stairs on hand, Mr. Waldron had to fetch his ladder for the crew, all of whom were anxious to leave a ship that had apparently developed a mind of its own. Phone calls were made and hospitality for the astronauts was divided between the two houses. Soon police sirens were heard, followed shortly by the sounds of fire engines and ambulances. Even though their services weren't needed, their drivers couldn't pass up the excitement.

By mid-morning the army arrived and blocked off the road, though that had been effectively done already by the imposing bulk of the spacecraft itself. Shortly afterward, flustered officials from NASA landed in a flock of helicopters.

The number of television and radio crews was increasing by the hour. Their helicopters chopped and whirred through the air, circled for good camera shots, then settled into the fields. Soon they and the media that had arrived by road surrounded the two farmhouses like swarming insects.

Much earlier on, however, there had been no observers. The astronauts and their hosts had been inside making perplexed phone calls and eating toast and coffee. Had any glanced out a window, a clump of willows would have screened their view of two children and a skunk hauling an odd-looking metal cylinder up the ladder into the shuttle's open hatch.

"Are you sure you've got this all figured out?" Jonathan had grumbled, palming sweat from his forehead. "When they launch these things down in Florida they've got great huge booster rockets and tons of fuel—solid and liquid. How can this doohicky of yours replace all that?"

Karen had been wondering the same thing but had been afraid to sound like a scientific dummy by asking it.

The skunk couldn't contribute much muscle power to the effort but puffed and wheezed prodigiously as he pushed his furry shoulders against the metal. "It's not my fault your people's ideas of propulsion are back in the stone age." They hauled it up another rung. "This ship's designed fine for space flight—a little clumsy, but it'll do. All those rockets, though"—he grunted as they cleared one more rung—"hopelessly primitive."

"So what's in this tin can of yours?" Jonathan asked, giving it an annoyed heave.

"I bet it's matter/antimatter," Karen ventured. She might not be a science whiz, but she did watch "Star Trek."

"Close," the skunk admitted. "More of a contained dimensional overlap. Pure matter/antimatter reactions are too volatile."

With a final shove, they hoisted the alien engine through the hatch. "Whew!" Stinker gasped. "You know, I once used a body that could have lifted that thing like a pebble. I never could have fit it in this ship, though. Let's roll the unit over there, and I'll start hooking it up."

"Need any help with that part?" Jonathan asked hopefully.

"No, that's a piece of cake. Speaking of which. . . ."

"Yeah, yeah, the peanuts," Karen said. "Let's haul up those grocery bags, Jonathan. Then we'd better get back. It'll look funny if we're not there, all agog over a house full of astronauts."

Shortly after the two children slipped back to their homes, one of the astronauts thought to come out and close the hatch against possible curiosity seekers. He never noticed the small black and white mammal tinkering quietly in the shadowy cabin.

Once the military had arrived, the area was cordoned off. It was midafternoon when a NASA engineer climbed Mr. Waldron's ladder intending to check out the shuttle controls.

Watching from her porch, Karen held her breath as the young man pushed open the hatch and disappeared inside. A moment's silence was broken by a blood curdling shriek. The man burst through the hatch and scrambled down the ladder coughing and fanning a hand in front of his face. Following right behind him came a cloud of noxious odor and a streak of black and white that darted down the ladder, through the legs of startled soldiers, and off into the woods.

The soldiers backed away from the reeking engineer who between coughs said, "The crazy thing must've climbed in when the hatch was open. The place stinks. Won't be able to go in for hours. Do I need a shower!"

He ran up onto Karen's porch. Karen held the door open with one hand, covering her face with the other, more to hide her giggles than to escape his odor. Her mother, on the phone with a radio reporter, wrinkled her nose, pointed to the bathroom down the hall, then continued her conversation. "Well, we were just finishing breakfast. . . ."

Karen closed the door and, with Sancho at her heels, wandered out toward the road. She wondered what had become of the school bus. The driver, she knew, was a very unflappable type. When he'd seen that the road was being used as a runway, he'd probably just decided to turn around and skip their stop. She bet that the kids already on the bus had been hopping mad that he'd turned away from all the action.

But not many local people were missing it now. The army had sent in reinforcements to keep back the steadily growing crowd. There was a rumor afloat that terrorists had somehow forced down the shuttle, though why they chose this particular stretch of soybean fields and farm-houses was not explained. People in the crowd kept looking sideways at each other, checking to see if anyone looked like a terrorist.

Karen's and Jonathan's families were allowed to re-main inside the cordoned off area. Karen wasn't sure if this was because they were under surveillance or be-cause they went with the houses. She suspected the latter. There didn't seem to be much of a thought-out security plan in effect, but then, this was hardly the sort of event anyone would have planned for.

From where she was, Karen could see a number of schoolmates outside in the crowd. She realized that ought to make her feel smug and important and was annoyed that it didn't. Adventures, she decided, may seem fine from a distance, but when they were actually happening to you they were mainly worry—and fear.

A military man, covered with meaningful-looking bits of braid and medals, was talking importantly to a television crew in front of Jonathan's house. Karen wandered over.

"The removal of the craft at this point is awaiting the arrival of the special truck designed to carry it. That has to come halfway across the country from the intended landing site, so it will be hours yet." At a reporter's question, he snapped, "No, I repeat, we have no idea why it landed here. The crew is being flown back to the Cape now for debriefing. And, of course, the ship and its computer will be thoroughly examined once it has . . . uh, aired out."

Just outside the security barriers, an enterprising lady was selling donuts and coffee from the back of her van. She was doing a booming business. Karen slipped up to Jonathan who was methodically licking maple frosting off his fingers.

"Did you see that NASA guy leave the ship?" she asked in a whisper.

Jonathan laughed conspiratorially. "I sure did. He acted like the devil himself was after him."

"Skunks do seem to have that effect on people," she giggled. "But why did Stinker leave, too? I mean, now he'll just have to sneak back in again."

"He thought at me in passing," Jonathan replied. "Said he'd finished hooking up his power unit and was off to get the others."

"Others? What did he mean by that?"

"Don't know. But he'd better be back before NASA's special truck gets here."

Another hour passed. It was beginning to get dark. The TV crews switched on their lights and flooded the stranded shuttle with unearthly white glare. Then the squeal of sirens was heard again on the road.

Karen and Jonathan hurried to see what was coming. State police cars were racing toward them, escorting a long, oddly arranged truck.

"That stupid skunk had better hurry," Jonathan yelled at her over the noise.

The TV crews moved in. The now haggard military man was explaining, "Yes, but it seems that the second truck with the loading equipment had a breakdown. It should be here shortly, though."

"Hurry up, Stinker!" Karen thought intensely, but she picked up no reply.

Retreating to her porch, she sat on a deck chair, then got up, went inside, and came back with a plaid blanket. The evening air was clear but carried a sharp autumn chill. Karen cocooned herself in the blanket and watched the bizarre scene around her. Despite her anxiety, her eyes kept closing. Last night's disturbed sleep was catching up with her.

Sounds and voices became illogically muddled. A warm, sleepy buzz wrapped around her. Distantly it was sliced into by exclamations. "Ooh, did you see that?" "Shooting stars!" "What a show we're getting tonight."

That's nice, Karen thought drowsily. Shooting stars.

Meteors, dropping to earth like . . . like spaceships! Her eyes flew open. She leaped to the front of the porch just in time to see the last of the shooting stars. A piercing arch of light, it cut through the purpling sky and disappeared beyond some distant trees.

Oh please, she thought, let it be just shooting stars.

Running off the porch, she pushed her way through the milling crowd of officials. One of them was frowning over some special-looking radio that was squawking at him about radar blips. She finally found Jonathan at the edge of one of his father's fields looking over the huge shuttle transport truck. Just then someone in the crowd behind them screamed.

"Eeek! Look out, a skunk!"

12

The Enemy

Karen and Jonathan spun around to see a streak of black and white shooting through the horrified crowd toward them. With its funny rippling run, it looked more like a huge caterpillar, but the thoughts Stinker shot at them were far from humorous.

"Come on, guys, I need help!"

"Zarnk?" Karen thought back fearfully.

"Yes, three ships. But I'll try to take care of them myself. I need your help with my recruits."

"Huh?"

"All those days, I was off recruiting more skunks. I figured Sylon High Command would find them and their spray very interesting. Last night, I told them all to wait in the clearing while I redid the engines. But the empty-heads scattered looking for grubs, and while I was rounding them up again the Zarnk landed. Now

I've got to try to sabotage their ships so they don't inter-fere with our escape. So I need you to lead the skunks back here and get them into the shuttle."

"Lead them back?" Jonathan objected. "They won't obey us. We can't mind-talk at *real* skunks."

"I've ordered them to follow you two unquestioningly wherever you lead. They're pretty obedient, unless they get hungry. So I've promised them a trove of goodies when they get where they're going. They'll follow. Now, hurry to the clearing. I'm off!"

He rippled off between several startled legs and disap-peared into the bushes. Karen and Jonathan looked around them. The crowd nearby had given them a wide berth, but many of the locals had heard about Karen's pet skunk, so the panic was muted.

With sheepish grins, the two slipped away from the staring eyes, then turned and ran furiously for the woods. As they neared the clearing, they slowed down.

"Do you think those skunks are really going to follow us when we get there?" Jonathan asked.

"If not, we're going to be the smelliest kids in three states."

Finally the trees thinned. In the deepening twilight, the ground of the clearing seemed alive, a seething, rippling carpet of black and white.

"Jeeze," Jonathan whispered, "There must be hun-dreds of them."

At the sound of his voice, everything shifted. A sea of black eyes glinted toward them.

"It's us," Karen said hesitantly. "Remember the ones

Stinker said you're to follow? Jonathan, I can't believe I'm actually trying to talk to skunks—real skunks!"

"Well, they haven't sprayed us yet. Let's try walking away and see what happens."

Slowly the two backed out of the clearing. With much rustling and random squeals and chirrups, the furry mob began to follow. Turning forward, Karen and Jonathan headed deliberately back toward their homes. Their little army moved with them until the two were in the middle of a steadily flowing black and white tide.

Suddenly they were within sight of the road, the brightly lit shuttle, and the enormous crowd.

"Courage," Karen said weakly after they'd both slowed to a halt. Jonathan squared his shoulders and jammed his glasses back along his sweaty nose. Then he reconsidered, slipped the glasses off, and stuffed them in a pocket. He had a feeling that if the faces around him were an unrecognizable blur, this whole incredible thing might be easier.

As they started forward, he muttered to Karen, "When this is all over, you realize we're going to be questioned by the CIA, FBI, NASA, and a whole bunch we don't even know about."

"At least that will get us out of school for a few days."

"Hmm."

"Maybe they'll take us someplace interesting."

"Like the torture chamber in the Pentagon basement."

"Oh, hush!"

Resolutely they marched on. People began to notice

them now. With startled screams they pushed back out of their way. Like a gust of wind, the screaming spread through the crowd, then was followed by a fearful silence. Everyone seemed frozen into inaction, afraid that any sudden move would set off a monumental stench.

Blushing violently but trying to ignore the onlookers, the two children lead their troops toward the shuttle. Skunk odor still wafted from the open hatch.

At the foot of the ladder, the two exchanged a few words, and Jonathan resolutely gripped the rungs and began climbing. With difficulty the skunks followed. Karen stayed at the bottom helping the smaller and clumsier animals. They really were not natural climbers. She concentrated fiercely on what she was doing, ignoring the rising chorus of exclamations and protests.

Several officials began moving toward them. The hindmost skunks turned nervously and began twitching their tails over their heads. Hastily the party retreated.

Cameras whirred, incredulous reporters whispered into microphones. One gruff voice was heard saying, "We've got to start shooting those varmits before they. . . ."

"Don't you dare!" whispered another. "That'll set them all off."

Above the mumbling, Karen caught her mother's voice but tried to tune it out. "Karen please, what are you? . . . Oh no, Sancho! Stay away from those skunks!"

Alarmed, Karen looked up. But Stinker must have given Sancho a parting command as well. The spaniel was sitting in front of the crowd, grinning and thumping his tail.

Suddenly another sound floated to her, one that seemed harmless enough—like the distant clatter of wind chimes.

13

Getaway

"Jonathan!" Karen cried, as she redoubled her efforts to boost skunks up the ladder, but she could see from Jonathan's pale wide-eyed face peering out from the hatch, that he had heard as well.

Gradually members of the crowd seemed to hear it too and began turning curiously toward the woods. "Great God in Heaven!" someone yelled. "What are those?"

Heads swiveled, voices screamed—screamed in absolute horror this time. People began pushing back from the fringe of trees. From out of the woods strode a cluster of poles held at the top by a pulsing gelatinous mass. Several other creatures clattered after it.

The things marched forward knocking down and stepping on panicky people in their path. A few soldiers and police hurriedly raised their guns and fired but with no noticeable effect. As if swatting flies, several Zarnk raised metal-tipped pole-arms, and a line of trucks in the army barricade vanished in an orange glow. Pandemonium.

"Look," Jonathan yelled from his vantage point, "one of them's carrying sort of a clear box. There's something black and white inside."

"They've captured Stinker!" Karen's cry could scarcely be heard over the chaos of gunshots and cries of the crowd.

"They're coming this way! Maybe they're after the shuttle, too. We've got to stop them!"

"We've got to save Stinker!"

Now a dozen of the creatures had cleared the woods. As people scrambled out of their way and soldiers fired at them, the aliens continued stalking toward the shuttle. The ship that had earlier looked so awesome and exciting suddenly seemed cold and alone in the white glare of abandoned TV lights.

Karen looked down at the small skunk kitten nuzzling in her arms. She'd been helping it up the ladder when the Zarnk appeared. Thoughtfully she put the little animal back on the ground. "Jonathan, what about the secret weapon?"

"Huh? Skunk spray? But *we* can't think at them to go spray the Zarnk. And Stinker's cage must be thought-proof, or he would have tried by now."

"I guess so. But . . . no, wait. He's *already* ordered them to follow us. All we have to do is lead the attack. Let's go!"

Jonathan stared aghast as Karen hopped over the skunks around her and ran down the road toward the advancing Zarnk. He glanced behind him at the agitated mass of black and white. "Okay guys, follow us!" He scrambled down the ladder. "Charge!"

With little grace but great vigor, skunks poured out of the ship and joined those still on the ground in pelting after the two children. At first the Zarnk ignored them—the little animals hardly looked threatening—but as the strange army drew closer, the lead Zarnk raised one of its poles. It pointed the glinting metallic tip at the leaders.

Karen and Jonathan, running abreast, skidded to a halt. In wide-eyed horror they looked at each other, then threw themselves to the asphalt. Confused, the skunks milled about. Suddenly leaderless, they were left to nothing but their instincts.

As the threatening Zarnk advanced, scores of skunks spun around. Here, clearly, was an enemy. Nearly in unison they raised their tails and shot an oily cloud of stench.

Startled silence fell on the fleeing humans and Zarnk alike. Then high piercing wails split the air. The tall Zarnk began staggering blindly about. Their tops whitened and flaked away, leaving their legs to fall like dry bones to the surface of the road.

A clear box fell from the grip of one and cracked open as it bounced over the asphalt. Dizzily, a black and white creature stumbled out.

The two children lay curled up on the road like sow bugs, but nothing could keep out the awful burning stench. Coughing, eyes clenched shut against the stinging spray, Karen wondered if it might not have been better to be zapped by a Zarnk ray gun.

"Nonsense," said a familiar voice in her mind. She felt a soft furry muzzle push against her face. Opening her tear-streaming eyes, she looked into a pair of black beady ones.

"Thanks, guys. That was some rescue. Those jerks thought I was one of this planet's big shots and were holding me hostage in exchange for the Sylon spy they thought was hiding here. Good thing they don't pick up minds too well. I don't know what they thought you humans were—wildlife maybe. But that ship must have looked just too good to leave alone."

"Oh, Stinker!" Karen said, barely able to talk for the gagging stench in the air. She picked the little creature up and hugged him.

Jonathan looked about, trying to ignore the withering bits of Zarnk. Those people who had not run completely away were standing at a distance, coughing and fanning their hands in the air, but a few soldiers were beginning to stumble back their way.

"We'd better get the little general and his army back to the shuttle. Skunks may stink, but they're not as permanently off-putting as those Zarnk guys."

"Stink?" Stinker thought indignantly. "I'll have you know. . . ."

"No, you won't," Karen said as, holding him tight, she scrambled to her feet and ran back up the road. "It's daring getaway time."

Under orders once more, the victorious skunks dutifully padded after the children. Soon they were again clambering into the shuttle. This time Stinker stood at the top directing operations while Karen and Jonathan both boosted skunks up the ladder.

The man with the medals was weaving his way toward them, a handkerchief to his nose. "See here, those creatures must get out of there. That's government property!"

"It's okay, sir," Jonathan shouted. "They're American skunks—most of them."

"If you kids don't stop that and tell us what on earth is going on. . . ." The man broke into a coughing fit and retreated as a new cloud of stench sailed his way.

"Time to go," Stinker said, lowering his tail. "Thanks for everything. You've been real friends, you know. Now, keep it up with each other if you can."

"Sure," Jonathan replied with a blush. The last little skunk left his hands and pulled itself up the ladder.

Karen looked up at the plump leader, incongruously majestic at the edge of the hatch. "Stinker, we'll miss you."

"Hey, don't be sad. This is a pretty fair planet, you know. I'll put in a glowing report when I get home. Maybe they'll set up trade relations or something."

"We can ship you tons of peanut butter," Karen said, trying to smile.

"Right! And in any case, I'll try and drop by here. You two ought to go on a *real* space adventure sometime. You're just the type for it. Oops, got to go."

A troop of soldiers was trotting their way, rifles in hand. Stinker dropped from sight and the hatch closed. Jonathan pulled away the ladder. "Got to get this back to my dad," he shouted as he and Karen ran off.

A few soldiers halfheartedly headed after them, then turned back and joined the others who were milling about the shuttle and banging on anything they could reach.

The bemedaled man, his uniform reeking of skunk, was stamping about, shouting, "How could those little beasts possibly close the door? How on earth are we going to get them out of there? What were. . . ."

Suddenly the ship shuddered. A rumble began deep within and built to a roar as the engine burst into life.

"It can't do that!" the man yelled hysterically as he and the others ran back from the noise and heat. "It can't start up like that!"

A reporter popped out of a bush where he'd been cowering with his cameraman. "Sir," he said, thrusting a microphone into the frazzled man's face, "can it take off from here?" He had to yell above the engine noise.

"Of course not, idiot! No booster rockets. It's not powered for it. And anyway, there's just a bunch of skunks in there, for crying out loud!"

White heat glowed from the engines, and slowly the shuttle moved forward. Purple with rage, the army man just stared and pointed. It rolled into the Waldrons' barnyard, turned around, and headed back up the road, gathering speed as it went.

An army roadblock of trucks stretched across the road ahead. The soldiers still manning the trucks leaped into the beanfields as the roaring spacecraft bore down upon them.

With a sudden burst of power, the shuttle's nose jerked upward, and the ship rose at an officially impossible angle into the sky.

From the Waldrons' front porch, Karen and Jonathan watched as it climbed into the night, a great white stripe against a field of soft black.

To Karen it looked familiar. "I wonder why no one ever named a constellation 'The Skunk?'"

"Maybe on another planet someone has," Jonathan suggested, "or will."

"And maybe we'll get a chance to find out someday."

The two friends looked at each other and grinned.